PENGUIN BOOKS
JI MANTRIJI
VOLUME 1

Jonathan Lynn was born in Bath, England in 1943. As well as winning awards for his writing he has enjoyed a prolific acting career in film, television and on stage. He now lives in Los Angeles, where he is a successful movie director.

Antony Jay was born in 1930 and has spent forty-five years travelling in the realms of government and politics as a television writer and producer. He has worked as an executive in British television, as well as on a number of successful political and royal documentaries, and most recently has edited the *Oxford Dictionary of Political Quotations*. He was knighted in 1988.

Alok Tomar has worked with *Jansatta* and *Aaj Tak*, and currently writes a syndicated column *Shabdartha*.

Monisha Shah was born in Bombay in 1969, and spent several years working in the television industry in India. Currently employed by BBC Worldwide, she was responsible for developing both the book and TV adaptation of *Ji Mantriji*. She is based in London and travels to India frequently on work, and to see her parents, sister and beloved dog, Humphrey.

Ji Mantriji

Volume 1

The Diaries of Shri Suryaprakash Singh

Based on the original
Yes Minister
By Jonathan Lynn and Antony Jay

Adapted and translated for Indian television by Alok Tomar
English version by Monisha Shah

PENGUIN BOOKS
in association with
BBC Worldwide

Penguin Books India (P) Ltd., 11 Community Centre, Panchsheel Park, New Delhi
110017, India
Penguin Books Ltd., 27 Wrights Lane, London W8 5TZ, UK
Penguin Putnam Inc., 375 Hudson Street, New York, New York 10014, USA
Penguin Books Australia Ltd., Ringwood, Victoria, Australia
Penguin Books Canada Ltd., 10 Alcorn Avenue, Suite 300, Toronto, Ontario M4V 3B2,
Canada
Penguin Books (NZ) Ltd., Cnr Rosedale & Airborne Roads, Albany, Auckland,
New Zealand

First published by Penguin Books India in association with BBC Worldwide 2001
Original edition of *Yes Minister* published by BBC Books, an imprint of BBC Worldwide
Ltd.

Copyright © Jonathan Lynn and Antony Jay 1981, 1982, 1983, 1984, 1989, 2001

10 9 8 7 6 5 4 3 2 1

Typeset in Sabon by Wordkraft Editorial Services, New Delhi
Printed and bound at Thomson Press (India) Ltd., New Delhi

This is an adaptation of the original *Yes Minister* books by Jonathan Lynn and Antony
Jay. This book is published to accompany the BBC television series *Ji Mantriji*, the
Hindi adaptation of the original BBC television series, *Yes Minister*, which was
produced for BBC Worldwide in India by NDTV for telecast on Star Plus.

This is a work of fiction. Names, characters, places and incidents are either the product
of the authors' imagination or are used fictitiously, and any resemblance to any actual
person, living or dead, events or locales is entirely coincidental.

CONTENTS

1
Khuli Sarkar
1

2
Bachat Abhiyan
31

3
Nehle Pe Dahla
63

4
The Hit List
93

5
The Foreign Visit
129

6
Raaz Ki Baat
163

7
Jaanne Ka Haq
193

1

Khuli Sarkar
(Open Government)

August 24th

Well, perhaps it's the early hours of Friday the 25th now. I am most excited. I have just been returned to Parliament from the Sevadham constituency. And after years of sitting in the Opposition, the Rashtriya Satya Dal has finally won a general election and we're in office.

After the result was announced I went to the RSD party's celebration party and saw Karan Thapar on TV say: 'And so Suryaprakash Singh's back, with an increased majority in his marginal constituency. After many years as a Shadow Minister in the Opposition he seems almost certain to get a Cabinet post in the new government.'

Prannoy Roy seemed doubtful, though. I do hope Karan Thapar's right.

August 25th

I'm still hoping but I wonder if Prannoy Roy knows something that I don't.

I've been sitting by the telephone ever since breakfast. No potential Cabinet Minister ever moves more than twenty feet from the telephone in the twenty-four hours following the appointment of a new Prime Minister. If you haven't heard within twenty-four hours, you're not going to be in the Cabinet.

Chandni kept me supplied with constant cups of tea all morning, and when I returned to the sofa next to the phone after lunch she asked me to help with the shopping if I didn't have anything else to do. I explained to her that I couldn't because I was waiting for the call.

'Who from?' Sometimes Chandni really is a bit dense.

The phone rang. I grabbed it. It was Dikshit, my special political adviser, saying that he was on his way over. I told

Chandni, who wasn't pleased.

'Why doesn't he just move in?' she asked bitterly.

Sometimes I just don't understand her. I patiently explained to her that, as my political adviser, I depend on Dikshit more than anyone. 'Then why don't you marry *him*?' she asked. 'I now pronounce you man and political adviser. Whom politics has joined let no wife put asunder.'

It is awfully difficult for Chandni, I know. Being an MP's wife is a pretty thankless task. But now that I may be a Minister, she'll at last reap the rewards!

The phone rang all day. Local party workers, the gas office, the plumber, Dikshit, all sorts of useless people ringing up to congratulate me. 'On what?' I said to Chandni. 'Don't they realize I'm waiting for the call?'

'Why don't you go for a walk and you can buy some vegetables for dinner on the way home?' She sounded tense.

I explained to Chandni that I simply didn't dare to leave the phone. Chandni betrayed her usual total lack of understanding. 'Look, if the PM wants you to be in the Cabinet, the PM will phone back if you're out. Or you can phone back.'

Chandni will never understand the finer points of politics. [*Suryaprakash was very insecure about his Cabinet prospects because he had previously run Harmohan Singh's campaign against the new PM, Bhaskardev, for the leadership of the RSD party. The question was whether the PM would be strong enough to ignore Suryaprakash Singh or whether, in the interests of party unity, the PM would be obliged to give him a good job.— Ed.*]

By the end of the day I heard on the grapevine that Pervaiz Khan Saheb's got Defence. Poor old Defence. Chandni wanted to know how he could be in charge of Defence if he can't tell the difference between a pistol and a machine gun. I explained to Chandni that as Raksha Rajya Mantri [*Minister for Defence—Ed.*], he will simply do some arms deals, take a few salutes at parades and make a few speeches about Pakistan and China. He will not actually fight in any war, so he is not expected to know anything about Defence, I said.

Narmada Babu's got the Prakritik Urja [*Natural Energy Resources—Ed.*] Ministry, in charge of Gobar Gas [*bio gas—Ed.*], as expected. Singh's got External Affairs, Sinha's got Labour and Jagannathanji will get Health.

I told Chandni of these appointments, and she asked me if anyone had got Brains. I suppose she means Education.

August 26th
At last I'm a Cabinet Minister. And today I had my first encounter with the Administrative Service, and I must say I am very impressed.

I got the call from Party HQ at about 9 a.m., after a sleepless night, and immediately Dikshit and I went to Race Course Road, where I was asked by the PM to take over the Ministry of Administrative Affairs.

This is an important post. In the Cabinet ranking, about eighth or ninth I should think. On the other hand, Singh reminded me (when he phoned to congratulate me) that the MAA is a political graveyard, a bit like the Home Ministry, and the PM may have over-promoted me—a vengeful move. I am determined to get a grip on the MAA and prove to the PM that I'm not so easily taken care of.

I was expecting to be Minister of Agriculture, as I've followed Agriculture for seven years, and have many good ideas about it, but for some inexplicable reason the PM decided against this.

[*We found a memo from Shri H.K. Sanghvi, Secretary of Agriculture, to Shri Jugran Dayal, Secretary to the Cabinet, imploring Shri Dayal to make sure that Suryaprakash did not get Agriculture as he was too 'knowledgeable' about it. Cabinet papers show that Shri Dayal managed to convey to the PM that it would be better for Suryaprakash not to go to Agriculture because 'he's been thinking about it rather too long and is perhaps in a bit of a rut'.—Ed.*]

An official car met me as I came out of Party HQ, and I was driven straight to the MAA. I was met on the front steps by Kaul, who is to be my Private Secretary. 'I am happy to be of service, sir, but if you'd prefer to replace me with someone of your own choice, someone like you . . .' he said. I vetoed the idea immediately. 'If he was someone like me, he would be a Minister himself,' I countered, feeling good-humoured. He seems a likeable enough chap. 'Thank you so much sir,' Kaul replied. 'From now on I will share your work, your troubles will be my troubles and your *ghaplas* will be my *ghaplas.*' ['*Ghapla' is Hindi for major blunders of the indisputable kind—Ed.*]

I think he meant genuine mistakes; after all Ministers too make mistakes I suppose.

To my surprise he instantly knew who Dikshit was, as we got out of the car, though he made a joke about 'digging etc.', which always infuriates Dikshit. [*Dikshit is pronounced Deeg-shit, which sometimes prompts inappropriate jokes of the lavatory kind—Ed.*]

We walked down miles of corridors. When we got to my office Dikshit had disappeared with the Assistant Private Secretary. Kaul assured me that Dikshit was being taken care of. They really are extremely nice and helpful.

My office is large, with a big desk, a conference table with lots of chairs around it, and a few armchairs arranged around a coffee table to form a conversation area. Otherwise, rather characterless. Kaul immediately offered some hospitality.

'A drink, Mantriji?'

I nodded. 'Suryaprakashji,' I said, as I want us to be on first-name terms.

'Gin?' he said, mishearing me.

'No,' I said, 'Suryaprakashji will be fine. Call me Suryaprakashji.'

Kaul said, 'If it's all right with you, I'd rather call you Mantriji, Mantriji.'

'Mantriji, Mantriji?' Then I realized what he meant. I asked him, 'Does that mean I have to call you Private Secretary, Private Secretary?'

Kaul said I was to call him Kaul. I'm sure that in the course of time I'll persuade him to call me Suryaprakashji.

A moment later Shri Rajnath Mathur arrived. He is in his early fifties I should think, but somehow ageless.

He welcomed me to the Department. Kaul introduced us.

'This is Shri Rajnath Mathur, Mantriji. He is the Secretary of the MAA, the Department Chief.'

'Bhai, if you are the Chief, then what am I doing here?' I joked, half-seriously.

'I am your Chief servant, sir,' Mathur replied.

He is charming and intelligent, a typical senior IAS officer.

'I believe you've met before,' Kaul remarked. I was struck for the second time by how well informed the young man was.

Mathur said, 'Yes, we did cross swords when the Mantriji gave me a grilling over the estimates in the Imports and Excise Committee last year. He asked me all the questions I hoped nobody would ask.'

This is splendid. Mathur clearly admires me. I tried to brush it off. 'Well,' I said, 'Opposition's about asking awkward questions.'

'Yes,' said Mathur, 'and government is about not answering them.' I was surprised. 'But you answered all my questions, didn't you?' I commented.

'I'm glad you thought so, Mantriji,' said Mathur. I didn't quite know what he meant by that. I decided to ask him who else was in the Department.

'Briefly, Mantriji, I am the Permanent Under-Secretary of State, known as the Secretary. Kaul here is your Principal Private Secretary. I, too, have a Principal Private Secretary, and he is the Principal Private Secretary to the Secretary. Directly responsible to me are twelve Additional Secretaries, forty Joint Secretaries, fifty-five Under-Secretaries and a hundred and twenty Deputy Secretaries. Directly responsible to the Principal Private Secretaries are Private Secretaries. The Prime Minister will be appointing two Parliamentary Under-Secretaries and you will be appointing your own Parliamentary Private Secretary.'

'So many Secretaries—can they all type?' I joked.

'None of us can type, Mantriji,' replied Mathur smoothly. 'Ms Nagpal types—she is your secretary.'

I couldn't tell whether or not he was joking. 'What a pity,' I said. 'We could have opened a typing agency.'

Mathur and Kaul laughed. 'Very good, Mantriji,' said Mathur. 'Most amusing, sir,' said Kaul. Were they genuinely amused at my wit, or just being patronizing? 'I suppose they all say that, do they?' I ventured.

Mathur reassured me on that. 'Certainly not, Mantriji,' he replied. 'Not quite all. But to go on, Mantriji, every officer in this Department deals with at least ten files a day.'

I did the calculations in my head, quite quickly I thought. 'But that makes a minimum of 2,000 files a day. Isn't that rather a large figure? Why so many . . .?'

Kaul explained, 'Sir, files to recommend the making of other files; once they are created, more files to recommend the movement of files; files to file files and finally files to show where those files are filed.' Silence ensued.

I decided to take charge at once. I sat behind my desk and to my dismay I found it had a swivel chair. I don't like swivel chairs. But Kaul immediately assured me that everything in the office can be changed at my command—furniture, decor, paintings, office routine and timings. I am unquestionably the boss!

Kaul then told me that they have two types of chairs in stock, to go with two kinds of ministers: 'One kind folds up instantly and the other goes round and round in circles.'

On second thoughts, perhaps that was another of Kaul's little jokes.

I decided that the time had come to be blunt and to tell them what's what. 'Frankly,' I said, 'this Department has got to cut through the whole of the stuffy Parliament bureaucracy. We need a new broom. We are going to throw open the windows and let in a bit of fresh air. We are going to reduce the red tape and streamline this creaking old bureaucratic machine. We are going to have a clean sweep. There are far too many useless people just sitting behind desks.'

I became aware at this point that *I* was actually sitting behind a desk, but I'm sure that they realized that I was not referring to myself.

I explained that we had to start by getting rid of people who just make work for each other. Mathur was very helpful, and suggested that I meant redeploying them—which, I suppose, is what I *did* mean. I certainly want to reduce overmanning, but I don't actually want to be responsible for putting people out of work.

But, by the clean sweep and the new broom, I meant that we must have a more Open Government—*Khuli Sarkar*. We had made election pledges about this, and I intend to keep them. We must take the nation into our confidence. I said all this to Mathur and Kaul who, to my surprise, were wholeheartedly in favour of these ideas.

Mathur referred to my speeches on this subject in Parliament last year. And he referred to my *India Times* article, the *News at Nine* interview, and the manifesto.

I was most impressed that he knew so much about me. Mathur then produced draft proposals, to implement my policies in a White Paper. I was flabbergasted. The efficiency of the Administrative Service is quite astounding. They even plan, Mathur tells me, to call the White Paper '*Khuli Sarkar*'.[*Open Government—Ed.*]

All of these draft proposals are available to me within thirty-six hours of the new government being elected and within minutes of my arrival at my office. And on a weekend! Remarkable chaps. I asked Mathur who had done all this.

'The creaking old bureaucratic machine,' he replied with a smile. 'No seriously, Mantriji, we are fully seized of the need for reform and we have taken it on board.'

I told him I was slightly surprised. 'I thought I'd have to fight you all the way,' I said. Mathur remarked that people have funny ideas about the Administrative Service.

'We are just here to help you formulate and implement your policies,' he explained.

He seems most sincere.

'But if you do all that, what will I do?' I asked.

'You will sign the papers, Mantriji. Attend press conferences, reply to questions raised in Parliament, participate in panel discussion on TV . . .'

'Really?! And to think that people believe that ministers are good-for-nothing fellows who waste valuable tax money. It's clearly hard work, isn't it?' I felt virtuous.

I asked Kaul what time I was expected in the office on Monday.

'Sir, anytime between 9 and 9.30 is fine,' he replied. 'But I will only be in around lunch—I have something important to do.'

'Important?' I questioned him, fully in charge.

'Sir, I need to go to the Housing Ministry to find a nice government bungalow for you in Lutyens' Delhi. After all, your manifesto states a home for every one, education for all. Now you may not need any education, but a house is quite essential.'

Truly, a likeable fellow.

As it's Saturday, we have arranged to start things properly on Monday morning. But they've given me six red boxes for the weekend, twenty files to be completed by tomorrow night— and more will be brought over by the driver tomorrow.

Kaul tells me that the previous Minister got a bit slack about the paperwork, especially during the election campaign. I'm certainly not going to be slack! I shall be a good Minister. I shall read everything they give me to read.

August 28th

I read all my boxes over the weekend. It took about nine hours. I was in the office by 9.20 a.m.

All the draft proposals for the *Khuli Sarkar* are superficially pretty impressive, but I happen to know that the Administrative Service is pretty good at delaying tactics. I mentioned this to Mathur at a meeting today. I think he's getting to know who's the boss around here.

But first things first. The day started with the diary. I found to my surprise that there were numerous appointments in it already. I asked how this was possible, since they didn't even know who would win the election.

Kaul said, 'We knew there'd be a Mantriji, Mantriji.' I told him not to start *that* again.

Mathur explained, 'India likes the business of government to continue, even when there are no politicians around.'

'Isn't that very difficult?' I asked.

'Yes . . . and no, Mantriji,' said Mathur. I must say, I can't see how it's possible to govern without the politicians. I'm afraid that Mathur might have delusions of grandeur.

My diary was pretty frightening. Cabinet at ten on Thursday. Nine Cabinet committees this week. A speech to the Law Institute tomorrow night, a deputation from the Indian Computer Association at 10.30 tomorrow morning, University Vice-Chancellor's lunch on Wednesday (another speech), inaugurating the Computer Software Exposition on Thursday morning (another speech), and so on.

I noticed that everything in the diary was in pencil, so presumably much of it can be and will be changed. I pointed out to Kaul that I have various other commitments.

Kaul looked puzzled. 'Such as?' he asked.

'Well . . . I'm on four policy committees of the party, for a start.'

'I'm sure you won't be wanting to put party before country,' said Mathur.

I had never looked at it in that light. Of course, he's absolutely right.

They were going to give me three more red boxes for tonight, by the way. When I grumbled a bit at this, Mathur explained that there are a lot of decisions to take and announcements to approve. He then tried something on, by saying, 'But we could, in fact, minimize the work so that you need only take the major policy decisions.'

I saw through that ploy at once. I insisted that I would take *all* the decisions and read *all* the relevant documents.

They've given me five boxes for tonight.

August 29th

Today I found that we have a problem with Dikshit. It's Tuesday today, and I realized that I hadn't seen him since I arrived at the MAA last Saturday morning.

To be quite truthful, I didn't actually realize it till he barged into my office, shouting and cursing, demanding to be let in.

It appears that he's been in the waiting room since Saturday. (I presume he went home on Sunday.) Kaul tried to tell him that he, Mathur and I were in a private conference, but I quickly sorted that out. I demanded that Dikshit, as my adviser, be given an office in the Department.

Mathur attempted to avoid the issue, saying that I had a whole Department to advise me now. Nonetheless I insisted.

'Well,' said Mathur, 'I believe we have some spare office space in Andheria Mor, don't we Kaul?'

Dikshit was appalled. 'Andheria Mor?'

'Yes, it's surprising, isn't it?' said Mathur agreeably. 'The government owns property all over Delhi.'

13

'But I don't want to be in Andheria Mor,' exclaimed Dikshit at the top of his voice.

'It's in a very nice part of Andheria Mor,' put in Kaul.

'And Andheria Mor's a very nice place. So I gather,' added Mathur.

Dikshit and I looked at each other. If they were not so charming and, well, gentlemanly, you might have thought they were trying to squeeze Dikshit right out.

'I need an office *here*, in this building,' said Dikshit, firmly and extremely loudly.

I nodded in agreement. Mathur capitulated at once, and told Kaul to find a suitable office right away. I then said that I expected Dikshit to have copies of all the papers that are given to me.

Kaul seemed surprised. 'All?'

'All,' I said.

Mathur agreed immediately. 'It shall be done—all the appropriate papers.'

In my opinion, these civil servants are not nearly so hard to deal with as people say. They are mostly very cooperative, and, even if not initially, always jump to it when spoken to firmly. I think I'm getting somewhere at last.

August 30th

After the last hectic four days, I have a little time to reflect—for posterity—on my first days in office.

First, I am impressed by the thorough grasp the officials at the MAA have of every situation. Second, how they are willing to cooperate fully, albeit under pressure, with Dikshit.

Thirdly, I am most struck by my dependence on these civil servants. I, like virtually all our new administration, knew nothing of the workings of Parliament except what I had learned second-hand. Because we have been so long in Opposition, only three members of the government, including the PM, have ever held office before. I had never seen the inside of a red box, never met a Permanent Secretary, and had no idea how things were really done.

This makes us more dependent on our officials than most new governments. Thank goodness they are behaving honourably.

[*That Monday, Shri Rajnath Mathur met Shri Jugran Dayal, Secretary to the Cabinet, at the Officers Club. Shri Mathur made a note about the meeting in his private diary.—Ed.*]

August 28   MONDAY

Jugran and I compared notes about the new government. His new Cabinet is scarcely distinguishable from the last one. My new Minister is learning the rules very quickly. I sounded Jugran out about the American Ambassador— rumour has it he has been spending a lot of time with the PM.

[*It is interesting to observe that senior civil servants, perhaps because they have spent thirty years writing notes in the margin of a memo or minute, only write in the margin even if there is nothing else on the page.—Ed.*]

15

Jugran and I compared notes about the new government. His new Cabinet is scarcely distinguishable from the last one. My new Minister is learning the rules very quickly. I sounded Jugran out about the American Ambassador—rumour has it he has been spending a lot of time with the PM.

Jugran confirmed this. But was unwilling to say whether it was about defence or trade. He is anxious about a leak—therefore it is imperative that the Cabinet doesn't hear about it yet.

I concluded, correctly, that it is defence *and* trade, i.e. the new aerospace systems contract.

The aerospace contract would be a considerable coup for the PM, less than two weeks after the election. Of course, it's been in the pipeline for months, but the new PM will obviously take the credit.

It will mean four and a half billion dollars, and many new jobs. All in marginal constituencies, too—what a coincidence!

This is valuable information. I gathered from Jugran that it would, therefore, be a grave embarrassment to the PM if a hypothetical Minister were to rock the Indo-American boat. Man overboard. The end of a promising new ministerial career, in fact.

Therefore, I have ensured that the Dikshit receives a copy of the invoice for the new American computers. Naturally he has not received it, because it is sensitive. But I think that this is the right moment.

I instructed my secretary to ensure that Dikshit find the invoice near the bottom of a pile. Let the man feel he has achieved something.

[*Kaul joined Shri Mathur and Shri Jugran Dayal at the club for an after-dinner coffee while they drank their after-dinner brandy —Ed.*]

I asked young Kaul what he makes of our new Minister. Kaul is happy. So am I. Suryaprakash swallowed the whole diary in one gulp and apparently did his boxes like a lamb last Saturday and Sunday. He'll be house-trained in no time.

All we have to do is head him off this *Khuli Sarkar* nonsense, I remarked to Kaul. Kaul said that he thought that we were in favour of Open Government. I hope I have not over-promoted young Kaul. He still has an awful lot to learn.

I explained that we are calling the White Paper '*Khuli Sarkar*' because you always dispose of the difficult bit in the title. It does less harm there than on the statute books.

It is the law of Inverse Relevance: the less you intend to do about something, the more you have to keep talking about it.

Kaul asked us, 'What's wrong with Open Government?' I could hardly believe my ears. Jugran thought he was joking. Sometimes I wonder if Kaul really is a flyer, or whether we shouldn't just send him off to a career in the Andaman and Nicobar Islands.

Jugran pointed out, with great clarity, that Open Government is a contradiction in terms. You can be open—or you can have government.

Kaul said that the citizens of a democracy have a right to know. We explained that, in fact, they have a right to be ignorant. Knowledge only means complicity and guilt. Ignorance has a certain dignity.

Kaul then said, 'The Mantriji wants a *Khuli Sarkar*.' Years of training seem to have had no effect on Kaul sometimes.

I remarked that one does not just give people what they want, if it's not good for them. One does not, for instance, give

17

whisky to an alcoholic.

Jugran rightly added that if people do not know what you're doing, they don't know what you're doing *wrong*.

This is not just a defence mechanism for officials, of course. Kaul must understand that he would not be serving his Minister by helping him to make a fool of himself. Every Mantriji we have would have been a laughing-stock within his first three weeks in office if it had not been for the most rigid and impenetrable secrecy about what he was up to.

Kaul is a Private Secretary. I am an Under-Secretary of State. The very word Secretary means one who can keep a secret.

Kaul asked me what I proposed to do. Naturally I did not inform him of my plans for Dikshit to make a great discovery. This would be putting too great a strain on Kaul's loyalty to Suryaprakash.

I asked Kaul if he could keep a secret. He said he could. I replied that I could, too.

[*Mathur Papers l4/QLI/9a*]

[*Suryaprakash was, of course, in complete ignorance of the meeting described above.—Ed.*]

September 4th

Dikshit came bursting into my office, waving a document, 'Have you seen this?' he enquired at four thousand decibels.

I was delighted that the civil servants were giving him all the papers now. I said so.

'They're not,' he said derisively. 'Not the *real* papers.'

'Which real papers aren't you getting?' I wanted to know.

'How do I know, if I'm not getting them?'

This is, of course, absolutely true. And I don't know what he can do about it. [*This, of course, is an example of what management consultants call the Light-in-the-Refrigerator Syndrome, i.e. is the light on when the door is shut? The only way to find out is to open the door—in which case the door is not shut any more. —Ed.*]

But Dikshit did not want to discuss his problems in getting necessary information out of the officials.

'They think they're sending me the rubbish. But look what I've found—oho, we've got them, we've got them by the necks.'

I still didn't know what he was talking about. Dikshit explained further.

'We've got Shri Rajnath-Bloody-Mathur and Mr Chamcha-Private-Secretary-Kaul just where we want them.'

He brandished a sheaf of papers under my nose. I *still* didn't know what he was talking about, but I do think he has a good sense of rhetoric—perhaps I should let him write the draft of my conference speech next year.

I made Dikshit sit down, and explain calmly. He has found some ordinary office invoices that have tremendous political significance. The MAA has apparently bought one thousand computer terminals, at Rs 1 lakh each. Ten crore rupees of the taxpayers' money. And they are made in America!

This is shocking. Mathur's been keeping very quiet about this. And I'm not surprised. We make computers in my own constituency, Sevadham. And we have rising unemployment. It is a scandal that the Administrative Service is not buying Indian.

I sent for Mathur. He was in meetings all day, but Dikshit and I will confront him with this tomorrow. I am deeply grateful to Dikshit. Mathur is going to be very surprised indeed that we have found out about this so fast.

September 5th

The meeting with Mathur was a total success.

I showed him the invoices for the computer terminals. He admitted that the MAA has purchased this brand for the whole of the government.

'But they're not Indian,' I pointed out.

'That is unfortunately true,' he agreed, somewhat shamefaced.

'We make these machines in India.'

'Not of the same quality,' he said.

This is very probably true, but naturally I can't admit it even if it is.

'They are better quality,' I said firmly. 'They come from my constituency.' I told Mathur to cancel the contract.

He responded that it was beyond his power to do so, and that it could only be cancelled by the Commerce Ministry. He said it would be a major change of policy for the Administrative Service to cancel contracts freely entered into. Especially with overseas suppliers.

He suggested (a trifle impertinently, I thought) that I should take it up in Cabinet. 'Perhaps they would postpone the discussion on the Middle East, or nuclear disarmament, to talk about office equipment.'

I could see that this was out of the question. I was faced with a dilemma. If it couldn't be cancelled, how was I to face my constituency?

'Why need they know?' asked Mathur. 'Why need *anybody* know? We can see that it never gets out.'

I was staggered. Couldn't Mathur see that to keep it quiet was directly contrary to our new policy of Open Government, to which he was as firmly committed as I?

Dikshit spelled out the only alternative. 'If the order can't be cancelled, it must be published.'

Mathur asked why. For a moment I couldn't quite think of the answer. But Dikshit saw it at once. 'Two reasons,' he explained. 'First, it's a manifesto commitment. Second, it'll make the last Minister look like a traitor.'

Two unanswerable reasons. I really am very grateful to Dikshit. And he is running rings around Mathur. Perhaps Mathur is not as clever as I first thought. He seemed very anxious about the idea of publication. 'But surely,' he said to Dikshit, 'you're not suggesting that the Minister should make a positive reference to this confidential transaction in a speech?'

'A speech!' said Diskhit. 'Of course! That's the answer.' This is a superb idea of Dikshit's. My speech at the inauguration of the Software Exposition will deal with this scandalous contract. And we will release it to the press in advance.

I said as much to Mathur. Dikshit said, 'There. Who's running the country now?' I felt his glee was a little juvenile, but quite understandable.

Mathur seemed even more worried. I asked him for his advice, which was totally predictable. 'I think it might be regrettable if we upset the Americans.'

Predictable, and laughable. I pointed out to Mathur, in no uncertain terms, that it is high time that someone jolted the Americans out of their commercial complacency. We should be thinking about the Indian poor, not the American rich!

Mathur said, 'Mantriji, if that is your express wish the Department will back you. Up to the hilt.' This was very loyal. One must give credit where it's due.

I said that indeed it was my express wish. Kaul then said he would circulate the speech, as soon as it was written, for

21

clearance.

This was new to me. I've never heard of 'clearance'. More bureaucracy and pointless paperwork. This matter has nothing to do with any other department. And if another department disagrees, they can say so publicly. That's what *Khuli Sarkar* is all about.

Mathur pleaded with me to circulate the speech, if only for information. At first I opposed this, but he argued—quite convincingly, I thought—that Open Government demands that we should inform our colleagues in government as well as our friends in the fourth estate.

My final word to Mathur, as the meeting concluded, was to see that the speech went straight to the press.

'Mantriji,' he said, 'we shall obviously serve your best interests.' A notable victory by Dikshit and me, in the cause of Open Government.

[*A typescript of Suryaprakash's 'Tryst with Destiny' like speech has been found in the files of the MAA. It is annotated with suggestions by Dikshit and Kaul, with comments from Suryaprakash.—Ed.*]

MINISTRY OF ADMINISTRATIVE AFFAIRS

SPEECH AT THE INAUGURATION OF THE SOFTWARE EXPO

A few days ago, we have made a pledge to the people about *Khuli Sarkar*—Open Government. So let us begin as we mean to go on. The people have a right to know what I know. And I have discovered that only last month the previous government signed a contract to import Rupees ten crores' worth of office equipment from America for use by the Administrative Service.

And yet an identical product— a better product—is made in India. By Indian workers. In Indian factories. So we are being fobbed off with second-rate American while Indian factories stand idle.

Well, if the Americans are going to take us for a ride, at least the Indian people have a right to know about it. And while I respect our friendship with America, I love my country and our computers more.

/over

September 8th

Today was disastrous. There have been some quite astounding turns of events.

My speech was completed. I was sitting in the office reading the press release when Kaul burst in with a minute from the PM's private office.

I have learned, by the way, that minutes, memos and submissions are all the same thing. Except that ministers send minutes to civil servants and to each other, whereas civil servants send memos and minutes to each other but submissions to ministers.

[*This is because a minute takes or orders action whereas a memo presents the background arguments, the pros and cons. Therefore, civil servants may send either to each other, as may politicians—but as a civil servant may not tell a Minister what to do he sends a submission, the very word designed to express an attitude of humility and respect. Minutes may, of course, also be notes about official meetings, and this meaning gives rise to the well-known Administrative Service axiom that meetings are where civil servants take minutes but politicians take hours.—Ed.*]

Anyway, the minutes made it clear that we were all to be very nice to the Americans for the next few weeks. I realized that my speech, which had gone out to the press, could not have been timed worse.

I was appalled. Not only by my bad luck. But I find it incredible that I, as a member of the Cabinet, should have no knowledge of forthcoming Defence agreements with the Americans. Whatever has happened to the doctrine of collective responsibility that I learned about at Doon and Gwalior?

September 4th

TO ALL DEPARTMENTS

To inform you that the Prime Minister is planning
a visit to Washington next month, and is anxious
that the visit will result in a valuable Indo-
American defence trade agreement. The importance
of this agreement cannot be overestimated.

Mathur then hurried into my office, looking slightly panicky. 'Sorry to burst in, Mantriji, but all hell's broken loose at PMO— apparently they've just seen your speech. They are asking why we didn't obtain clearance.'

'What did you say?' I asked.

'I said that we believe in Open Government. But it seemed to make things worse. The PM wants to see you in his office, right away.'

I realized that this could be the end for me. I asked Mathur what was likely to happen. Mathur shrugged.

'The Prime Minister giveth—and the Prime Minister taketh away.'

I left the room feeling sick. As I started down the corridor I thought I heard Mathur add, '*Pradhan Mantriji ki jai ho.*' But I think I must have imagined that.

[*Pradhan Mantriji ki jai ho is the Hindi equivalent of 'Blessed be the name of the Prime Minister'—Ed.*]

Mathur, Dikshit and I hurried down. We went straight to the House. I was to meet the PM in his office.

We were kept waiting for some minutes outside the PM's room. Then Diwansaheb, our Chief Whip, emerged. He came straight over to me.

'You're a real pain in the arse, aren't you? Did you write that idiotic speech? Have you lost your mind?' Diwansaheb really does pride himself on his dreadful manners. 'The PM's going up the wall. Hitting the roof. You can't go around making speeches like that.'

'It's *Khuli Sarkar*,' said Dikshit.

'Shut up, who asked you?' retorted Diwansaheb. Rude bugger. Typical Chief Whip.

I sprang to Dikshit's defence. 'He's right, Diwansaheb. It's *Khuli Sarkar*. It's in our manifesto. One of our main planks. The PM believes in Open Government too.'

'Open, yes,' said Diwansaheb. 'But not gaping.' Very witty! 'In politics,' Diwansaheb went on relentlessly, 'you've got to learn to say things with tact and finesse—and keep your trap shut too, at times!'

I suppose he's got a point. I felt very sheepish, but partly because I didn't exactly enjoy being ticked off in front of Mathur and Diskhit.

'How long have you been a Mantri?' Diwansaheb asked me. Bloody silly question. He knows perfectly well. He was just asking for effect.

'Nine days,' I told him.

'Then I think you may have earned yourself a place in the *Guinness Book of Records*,' he replied. 'I can see the headlines already—CABINET SPLIT ON US TRADE. SURYAPRAKASH LEADS REVOLT AGAINST PRIME MINISTER. That's what you wanted, is it?'

And he walked away.

Then Shri Jugran Dayal, the Cabinet Secretary, came out of the PM's office. Mathur asked him what news there was.

Shri Dayal said the same things, only in Parliament language. 'That speech is causing the Pradhan Mantriji some distress. Has it definitely been released to the press?'

I explained that I had given express instructions for it to go out at twelve noon. Shri Jugran seemed angry with Mathur. 'I'm appalled at you,' he said. I've never heard one civil servant express himself so strongly to another. 'How could you allow your Minister to put himself in this position without going through the proper channels?'

Mathur turned to me for help. 'The Mantriji and I,' he began, 'believe in Open Government. We want to throw open the windows and let in a bit of fresh air. Isn't that right, Mantriji?'

I nodded, but couldn't speak. For the first time, Shri Jugran addressed me directly.

'Well, Mantriji, it's good party stuff but it places the PM in a very difficult position, personally.' That, in Shri Jugran's language, is about the most threatening thing that has ever been said to me.

'But . . . what about our commitment to *Khuli Sarkar*?' I finally managed to ask.

'This,' replied Jugransaheb drily, 'seems to be the closed season for *Khuli Sarkar*.'

Then Mathur voiced my worst fears by murmuring quietly,

'Do you want to give thought to a draft letter of resignation? Just in case, of course.'

I know that Mathur was just trying to be helpful, but he really doesn't give much moral support in a crisis.

I could see that there was only one possibility left. 'Can't we hush it up?' I said suddenly.

Mathur, to his credit, was completely baffled by this suggestion. He didn't even seem to understand what I meant. These civil servants really are rather *buddhu*. [*Buddhu is Hindi for stupid —Ed.*]

'Hush it up?' he asked.

'Yes,' I said. 'Hush it up.'

'You mean,' Mathur was apparently getting the idea at last, 'suppress it?'

I didn't exactly care for the word 'suppress', but I had to agree that that was exactly what I did mean.

Mathur then said something like, 'I see. What you're suggesting is that, within the framework of the guidelines about Open Government which you have laid down, we should adopt a more flexible posture.' Civil servants have an extraordinary genius for wrapping up a simple idea to make it sound extremely complicated.

On second thoughts, this is a real talent that I should learn to cultivate. His phrasing might help me look as though I am not changing my posture at all.

However, we were saved by the bell as our saviour galloped over the horizon in the shape of Kaul hurrying into the waiting-room.

'About the press release,' he began breathlessly. 'There appears to have been a development which could precipitate a reappraisal of our position.'

At first I didn't quite grasp what that meant. But he then went on to say that the Department had failed to rescind the interdepartmental clearance procedure, which meant that the supplementary stop-order came into effect, which meant that it was *all right*!

In other words, my speech didn't go out to the press after all. By an amazing stroke of good luck, it had *only* been sent to the Prime Minister's Private Office. The Duty Office at the MAA had never received instructions to send it out *before* it was cleared with the PM and the External Affairs Ministry. Because of the American reference.

This wonderfully fortunate oversight seems to have saved my skin. Of course, I didn't let Mathur see my great sense of relief. In fact, he apologized.

'The fault is entirely mine, Mantriji,' he said. 'This procedure for holding up press releases dates back to before the era of *Khuli Sarkar*. I unaccountably omitted to rescind it. I do hope you will forgive this lapse.'

In the circumstances, I felt that the less said the better. I decided to be magnanimous. 'That's quite all right Mathursaheb,' I said. 'After all, we all make mistakes.'

'Ji Mantriji,' said Mathur.

2

Bachat Abhiyan
(The Economy Drive)

September 11th

On the train going up to Delhi after a most unrestful weekend in the constituency, I opened up the *Mid-Morning*. There was a huge article making a personal attack on me.

Let's Get Rid of Suryaprakash Singh

By Mohan Rajput
Special Investigator

The Minister for Administrative Affairs, Suryaprakash Singh, promised to carry out the government's pledge to slim down the Administrative Service, to wipe out interference from the Babus. But how many people realize that the Administrative Service is in fact growing every day?

I have discovered that no less than four Ministries check the supply of the same army uniforms. The Ministry of Defence checks to see that they get what they have ordered. The Ministry of Textiles checks to see that they have been manufactured according to government regulations. The Civil Supplies Ministry checks that the manufacturer falls in with the required standards, the Finance Ministry checks the bills and Suryaprakash Singh's mob just checks up on everybody else!

Suryaprakash Singh is the most obvious case of overmanning in the Indian government. Let's start by getting rid of him and saving at least one salary.

I looked around the train. Normally the A/C compartment is full of people reading the *Times of India*, the *Hindustan Times*, or the *Indian Express*. Today they all seemed to be reading the *Mid-Morning*.

When I got to the office Kaul offered me the paper and asked me if I had read it. I told him I had. Kaul told me that Dikshit had read it, and wanted to see me. Then Dikshit came in and asked me if I had read it. I told him I had.

Dikshit then read it to me. I don't know why he read it to me. I told him I had already read it. It seemed to make him feel better to read it aloud. It made me feel worse.

I wondered how many copies they sell every day. 'Two lakhs, three lakhs?' I asked Kaul.

'Oh *no*, Mantriji,' he answered, as if my suggested figures were an utterly outrageous overestimate.

I pressed him for an answer. 'Well, how many?'

'Um . . . four lakhs,' he said with some reluctance. 'So only . . . twelve lakh people have read it. Twelve or fifteen at most. And lots of their readers can't really read, you know.'

Dikshit was meanwhile being thoroughly irritating. He kept saying, 'Have you read this?' and reading another appalling bit out of it. For instance: 'Do you realize that more people serve in the Income Tax Department than the Border Security Force?' This came as news to me, but Kaul nodded to confirm the truth of it when I looked at him.

'Perhaps,' said Dikshit, still reading aloud from that bloody paper, 'the government thinks that a tax is the best form of defence.'

Kaul sniggered, then saw that I was not amused. He tried to change his snigger into a cough.

Dikshit then informed me, as if I didn't already know, that apart from the fact that my photo is positioned right next to the tea and underwear ads, this article is politically very damaging, and that I had to make slimming down the Administrative Service a priority. There's no doubt that he's right, but it's just not that easy.

I pointed this out to Dikshit. 'You know what?' he said angrily. 'You're house-trained already.'

I don't deign to reply. Besides, I couldn't think of an answer. [*The Administrative Service phrase for making a new Minister see things their way is 'house-training'. When a Minister is so 'house-trained' that he automatically sees everything from the Administrative Service point of view, this is known in Rajneeti terms as the Minister having 'gone native'.—Ed.*]

Mathur came in, brandishing a copy of the *Mid-Morning*. 'Have you read this?' he began.

This was too much. I exploded. 'Yes. Yes! Yes!!! I have read that stupid newspaper. I have read it, *you* have read it, *we have all bloody read it*. DO I MAKE MYSELF CLEAR?'

'Abundantly, Mantriji,' said Mathur coldly, after a brief pained silence.

I recovered my temper, and invited them all to sit down. 'Mathursaheb,' I said, 'we simply *have* to slim down the Administrative Service. How many people are there in this Department?'

'This Department?' He seemed evasive. 'Oh well, we're very small.'

'How small?' I asked, and receiving no reply, I decided to hazard a guess. 'Two thousand? . . . Three thousand?' I suggested, fearing the worst.

'About thirty-five thousand, I think, Mantriji?'

I was staggered. Thirty-five thousand people? In the Ministry of Administrative Affairs? Thirty-five thousand administrators, all to administer other administrators?

'Ji Mantriji . . . that's not including all those on temporary and daily wage contracts,' Mathur continued.

'We'll have to do an O&M,' I said. [*Organization and Method Study —Ed.*] 'See how many we can do without.'

'We did one of those last year,' said Mathur blandly. 'And we discovered we needed another five hundred people. However, Mantriji, we could always close your Special Bureaucratic Vigilance Committee.' [*The Special Bureaucratic Vigilance Committee was an innovation of Suryaprakash's, to which members of the public were invited to report any instances of excessive government bureaucracy which they encountered personally. It was disbanded after four months.— Ed.*]

I had been expecting this. I know Mathur doesn't like the Committee. How could he? But we are not cutting it. Firstly, it's a very popular measure with the voters. And secondly, it's the only thing I've achieved since I've been here.

'It is a chance for the ordinary citizen to help us find ways to stop wasting government money,' I reiterated.

'The public,' said Mathur, 'do not know anything about wasting public money. We are the experts.'

I grinned. 'Can I have that in writing?'

Mathur got offended. 'You know that's not what I meant,' he snapped. 'The Vigilance office is merely a troublemakers' letter box.'

'It stays,' I replied.

We gazed at each other, icily. Finally Mathur said, 'Well, off-hand, I don't know what other economies to suggest.'

This was ludicrous. 'Are you seriously trying to tell me,' I asked, 'that there's nothing we can cut down on?'

He shrugged. 'Well . . . I suppose we could do without one or two of the waiters in the canteen.'

I exploded again. I told him not to be ridiculous. I told him

I wanted facts, answers. I listed them:
1 How many people work here?
2 What do they all do?
3 How many buildings do we have?
4 Who and what is in these buildings?

I spelt it out. I demanded a complete study. First of all we'll put our own house in order. Then we'll deal with the rest of the departments. With a complete study, we'll be able to see where to cut costs, cut staff, and cut procedures.

Mathur listened with some impatience. 'The Indian Administrative Service, Mantriji,' he responded when I paused for breath, 'merely exists to implement legislation that is enacted by Parliament. So long as Parliament continues to legislate for more and more control over people's lives, the Administrative Service must grow.'

'Ha!' Dikshit made a derisive noise.

Mathur turned towards him with a glassy stare. 'Am I to infer that Dikshitji disagrees with me?'

'Ha!' repeated Dikshit.

Dikshit was getting on my nerves too. 'Dikshit, either laugh thoroughly, or not at all,' I instructed.

'Mantriji,' Mathur stood up. 'I am fully seized of your requirements, so if you'll excuse me I think I had better set the wheels in motion.'

After Mathur left Dikshit told me that there was a cover-up going on. Apparently the Urban Development Ministry has achieved cuts of Rs 80 crores in that Ministry alone. And the Administrative Service has suppressed news of it. I asked why. 'They don't want cuts,' said Dikshit impatiently. 'Asking Mathursaheb to slim down the Administrative Service is like asking an alcoholic to blow up a distillery.'

I asked Kaul if this story was true. Kaul said that he didn't know, but, if it was, he would be aghast. I asked them both to check up on it. Kaul said he'd find out through the grapevine, and I arranged with Dikshit to do some more digging.

[*Sometime in the next few days Kaul had an interview with Shri Rajnath Mathur. Shri Mathur wrote a memo following the meeting, which we found in the MAA Personnel Files —Ed.*]

> Kaul came at 5.15 p.m. to discuss the Rs 80 crores saved by the Urban Development Ministry. I remarked that I was aghast.

Kaul came at 5.15 p.m. to discuss the Rs 80 crores saved by the Urban Development Ministry. I remarked that I was aghast.

Kaul said he also was aghast, and that it was incredible that we knew nothing of this.

He sometimes reveals himself as worryingly *seedha* [*naïve —Ed.*]. I, of course, know all about it. I am merely aghast that it has got out. It might result in our getting less money from the Treasury in next year's PESC review. [*PESC is the Public Expenditure Scrutiny Committee —Ed.*]

I felt I would learn more about Kaul if I made the conversation informal. [*To do so, Shri Mathur would have moved from behind his desk to the conversation area, remarking that it was after 5.30 p.m. and offering Kaul a coffee —Ed.*] Then I asked him why he was looking worried. He revealed that he genuinely wanted the MAA to save money.

This was shocking. Clearly he has not yet grasped the fundamentals of our work.

There has to be some way to measure success in the Service. Indian Automobiles can measure success by the size of its profits. [*Indian Automobiles was the name of the car manufacturer into which crores of rupees of Indian taxpayers' money was paid in the 1980s in an attempt to produce employment in the Hindi cow belt. To be more accurate, IA measured its failure by the size of its losses.—Ed.*] However, the Administrative Service does not make profits or losses. Ergo, we measure success by the size of our staff and our budget. By definition a big department is more successful than a small one. It seems extraordinary that Kaul could have passed through the UPSC training without having understood that this simple proposition is the basis of our whole system.

Nobody had asked the Urban Development Ministry to save Rs 80 crores. Suppose everybody did it? Suppose everybody started saving money irresponsibly all over the place?

Kaul then revealed another curious blind-spot when he advanced the argument that the Mantriji wanted cuts. I was obliged to explain the facts of life:

1 Mantrijis come, and Mantrijis go. The average Mantri lasts less than eleven months in any Department.

2 It is our duty to assist Mantriji to fight for the Department's money despite his own panic reactions.

3 However, Mantriji must be allowed to panic from time to time. Politicians like to panic. They need activity—it is their substitute for achievement.

4 The argument that we must do everything a Mantri demands because he has been 'democratically chosen' does not stand up to close inspection. MPs are not chosen by 'the people'—

they are chosen by the leaders of the local unit of the party, i.e. thugs and hoodlums, and a handful of state unit supremos. The further 'selection' process is equally a nonsense: there are only 544 MPs and a party with just over 270 MPs forms a government—and of these 270, 100 belong to the dissenting factions, 50 are too old and too silly to be ministers, and 50 too young and too callow. Therefore there are about 70 MPs to fill 70 government posts. Effectively no choice at all.

5 It follows that as Mantris have had no proper selection or training, it is our patriotic duty to arrange for them to make the right decision as often as possible.

I concluded by teaching Kaul how to explain the saving of Rs 80 crores to Mantriji. I offered the following possibilities. Say that:

(a) they have changed their accounting system in that Ministry,

or (b) redrawn the boundaries, so that this year's figures are not comparable,

or (c) the money was compensation for special extra expenditure of Rs 20 crores a year over the last two years, which has now stopped,

or (d) it is only a paper saving, so it will all have to be spent next year,

or (e) a major expenditure is late in completion, and therefore the Ministry will be correspondingly over budget next year [*known technically as phasing —Ed.*],

or (f) there has been an unforeseen but important shift of personnel and industries to other regions whose expenditure rose accordingly,

or (g) some large projects were cancelled for reasons of economy early in the accounting period with the result that the expenditure was not incurred but the budget had already been allocated.

Kaul seemed to understand. I am concerned that he has not had adequate training so far. I intend to keep a close watch on him because, in spite of all this, I still think he shows promise.

He volunteered information that Dikshit was digging. Naturally, I arranged a government car to assist him. [*It is standard Administrative Service practice to provide government cars for troublesome outsiders. The driver would, at the very least, be relied on to report where he had been, if only to account for the mileage.*

Drivers are one of the most useful sources of information in Delhi. Their passengers are frequently indiscreet, forgetting that everything they say in the back seat can be overheard from the front. Furthermore, Ministers tend to forget confidential documents, and leave them behind in the car.

Information is the Indian Administrative Service's most valuable currency. Drivers barter information.—Ed.]

[*The following series of memos between Shri Rajnath Mathur and Shri Vijay Raman were found in a Ministry file —Ed.*]

A note from Shri Vijay Raman, Permanent Secretary to the Finance Ministry:

MINISTRY OF FINANCE

From the Secretary

Dear Mathur

Am concerned that your Minister is still trying to economize pointlessly.

VR

From the Secretary

Dear VR

Am hoping it will be like all the other government economy drives three days of press releases, three months of ministerial memos and file movements, then a crisis in Nepal, and back to normal again.

RM

From the Secretary

Dear Mathur

Hope you're right, but why take chances? I suggest another Operation Tapasya and Balidaan: 'Economy begins at home. Set a personal example. Can't expect others to do what we don't do ourselves,' etc.

VR

[*Tapasya and Balidaan—self-discipline and sacrifice—Ed.*]

From the Secretary

Dear VR

Good idea. Will try it. Thanks. Self-denial is probably the answer, as always.

RM

P.S. See you at the Culture Secretary's dinner at the IIC.

[IIC is short for India International Centre, in Delhi, where all the 'intellectual elite' of academia, arts and the civil service hang out —Ed.]

[*Suryaprakash's diary continues —Ed.*]

September 19th

Today we had the big meeting on expenditure cuts. Dikshit has been 'digging' for a couple of weeks. The meeting didn't actually end the way I thought it would, but we do now have a real programme of action, though not the one I expected.

At the meeting were Mathur, Kaul, and Dikshit who had come up with what seemed to be some astounding revelations about wastage in our midst. I told Mathur that he would be pretty surprised by it all, and that the new facts seemed to be a frightening indictment of bureaucratic sloppiness and self-indulgence.

Mathur seemed very concerned and intrigued, and was eager to learn where there might be scope for dramatic economies.

Dikshit had prepared two files, one on manpower and one on buildings. I decided to look at buildings first.

'Patel Bhavan,' I began. 'Sardar Vallabhbhai Patel Marg.'

'A huge building,' said Dikshit, 'with only a handful of people working there.'

Mathur said he happened to know about Patel Bhavan. 'It is certainly underused at the moment, but it is the designated office for the new Commission for Parliamentary Proposal Disposal. We're actually wondering if it'll be big enough when all the staff move in.'

This seemed fair enough. So I went on to Sarojini Bhavan, Patparganj. It is totally empty.

'Of course,' said Mathur. I asked him what he meant.

'Security, Mantriji. I can say no more.'

'Do you mean RAW?' I asked, confusedly.

Mathur shook his head, and said nothing. So I asked him

what he did mean.

'Under the National and Official Secrets Act, Mantriji, we do not admit that RAW exists,' he replied.

I had never heard anything so daft. I pointed out that absolutely everyone knows that it exists.

'Nevertheless, we do not admit it. Not everyone around this table has been vetted.'

Vetted is such a silly expression. I remarked that it sounds like something you do to cats.

'Yes, but not to political animals, Mantriji,' said Mathur sharply, eyeing Dikshit. 'Sarojini Bhavan is top secret.'

'How,' I asked sarcastically, 'can a seven-storey building in Patparganj be a secret?'

'Where there's a will there's a way,' replied Mathur, with (I think) a twinkle in his eye. It was all quite amicable, but I could see that he had no intention of discussing anything that had remotely to do with security while Dikshit was present. I had no intention of asking Dikshit to leave, so, reluctantly, I was forced to move on to the next two white elephants.

'Subhash Bhavan, Lal Qila Road. Estimated value, seventy crore rupees. Shankar Estate, prime property on Ring Road, estimated value, two hundred and thirty crores. Both buildings with a tiny staff, and entirely full of filing cabinets.'

'May I ask the source of these valuations?' Mathur enquired.

'Going rate for office property in the area,' said Dikshit.

'Ah. Unfortunately,' said Mathur in his most helpful tone, 'neither building would actually fetch the going rate.'

I asked why not.

'Subhash Bhavan has no fire escape or fire doors and the fabric of the building would not stand the alteration, so it can't be sold as offices.'

47

'Then how can we use it?' enquired Dikshit aggressively.

'Government buildings do not need fire safety clearance.'

'Why?' demanded Dikshit.

'Perhaps,' Mathur offered, 'because India's civil servants are not easily inflamed.' This time he chuckled. Another of his little jokes. He seemed to be increasingly pleased with himself. I didn't care for this.

We were not getting very far with our economies, so I asked why Shankar Estate couldn't be sold as offices.

'That,' said Mathur, 'has a three-level reinforced-concrete basement.'

'So?' I said.

'It is there in case,' said Mathur. I waited for him to complete his sentence, but after a while it became apparent that he thought he had already done so.

'In case?' I asked eventually.

'You know, Mantriji,' he said, his voice pregnant with hidden meaning. 'Emergency Government Headquarters, if and when.'

I was baffled. 'If and when what?'

Mathur was now at his most enigmatic. 'If and when . . . you know what,' he replied so quietly that I could hardly hear him.

'What?' I wasn't sure I'd heard correctly.

'What?' Now Mathur seemed confused.

'What do you mean, if and when you know what? If and when, I know what—what?'

At last Mathur decided to make his meaning clear. 'When the chips are down, Mantriji, and the balloon goes up and the lights go out . . . there has to be somewhere to carry on government, even if everything else stops.'

I considered this carefully for a few moments. 'Why?' I asked.

Mathur appeared to be absolutely staggered by this question.

He explained to me, as if I were a five-year-old, 'Government doesn't stop merely because the country's been destroyed. Annihilation is bad enough, without anarchy to make it even worse.'

Obviously Mathur was concerned about the danger of a lot of rebellious cinders.

However, this is clearly an MoD matter [*Ministry of Defence matter —Ed.*] and I can see it is beyond *my* power to do anything about Shankar Estate.

There was one more virtually unused building on Dikshit's list. It was my last shot. 'What about the Central Plaza building?' I enquired, without any real hope.

'Built for research into fish farming but we couldn't create a lake—no planning permission,' said Mathur, with the bland smile of a man who knows he's won five rounds and is way ahead on points.

Dikshit suddenly intervened. 'How does he know all this?' he enquired belligerently, and turned accusingly to Mathur. 'You *knew* where I had been.'

This hadn't occurred to me, but Dikshit was obviously right. I was about to question Mathur on that score, when Mathur said to me, most disarmingly, 'Of course we knew where he had been. Why, was he supposed to be spying?'

I wasn't ready for that particular googly. I realized at once that I was on a very sticky wicket.

Mathur pressed home his advantage. 'I mean, we *do* believe in Open Government, don't we?'

There was no answer to this, so, in my most businesslike fashion, I closed the Buildings file. [*In any case, it would have been impossible to sell all these government buildings simultaneously.*

If you put government property in Delhi on the market all at once, you would destroy the market—like diamonds —Ed.]

I turned to Manpower. Here, I felt I was on rock-solid ground. 'Apparently,' I began, 'there are ninety civil servants in Development Planning (North-East) exactly duplicating the work of one hundred and twenty others here in the Ministry of Planning.'

Mathur nodded. 'That stems from a Cabinet decision. Job creation in the North-East.'

At last we were in agreement about something. 'Let's get rid of them,' I proposed.

Dikshit chimed in eagerly, 'Yes, that would get rid of ninety civil servants at a stroke.' Somehow, the way Dikshit spits out the words 'civil servants' makes them sound more contemptible than petty thieves. If I were a civil servant I think Dikshit's style would offend me, though Mathur doesn't seem too bothered, I must say.

But he picked up Dikshit's phrase 'at a stroke'. [*Actually, Morarji Desai's phrase, originally applied to price reductions which, needless to say, never occurred —Ed.*] 'Or indeed,' said Mathur, 'at a strike.'

'What?' I said.

'Personally, Mantriji, I should be wholeheartedly in favour of such a move. A considerable economy. But . . . I should remind you that it is a depressed area. Hence the original job creation scheme. It would show great political courage for the government to sack staff in a depressed marginal constituency.'

We sat for a while in silence. I must say, I think it was rather sporting of Mathur to remind me that a marginal constituency was at stake. Normally civil servants take no interest in these vital political calculations.

Clearly, I couldn't possibly risk a strike up there. But I was feeling really hopeless about these economies by now. I decided to put the ball back into Mathur's court.

'Look, Mathur,' I said, 'this is all very well . . . but . . . well, I just don't believe that there are no savings to be made in the Administrative Service. I see waste everywhere.'

'I agree with you, Mantriji,' came the reply, much to my surprise. 'There is indeed scope for economy . . .'

'Then . . .' I interrupted, '. . . *where*, for God's sake?' And to my surprise, Mathur suddenly became very positive.

'I sometimes feel that the whole way we do things is on too lavish a scale. You know, cars, furnishings, private office staff, entertainment, photo-copying machines, computers . . .'

This was marvellous. I couldn't agree more. I nodded enthusiastically.

'There is a difficulty, however,' he added. My heart sank again, but I waited to hear what it was. 'It does cause profound resentment if those at the top continue to enjoy the convenience and comforts they have withdrawn from those below them, not to mention the deeply damaging publicity . . .'

He broke off, and waited to see how I would react. I wasn't awfully keen, I must admit. It became clear that Mathur's scheme was that he and I should set a personal example. Economy begins at home, and we can't expect others to do what we don't do ourselves, and so forth.

I challenged Mathur. 'Would it really save that much?'

'Directly, no,' he said. 'But as an example to the whole public service . . . incalculable!'

Then Dikshit came up with the decisive argument in favour of Mathur's plan. He pointed out that there would be lots of great publicity in it. He suggested the sort of newspaper headlines

51

we'd be getting: THE MINISTER SHOWS THE WAY, or SLIMLINE GOVERNMENT, SINGH SETS EXAMPLE. We might even get a first-name headline: SAVE IT, SAYS SURYAPRAKASH.

I gave Mathur the go-ahead to put the scheme into practice as soon as possible. I shall be interested to see how it works. At this moment, I have high hopes.

September 24th
Sunday morning. I'm writing this at home, at Sevadham.

Haven't had time to make any entries in the diary for some days because this economy drive is creating a lot of extra work for me. However, I'm sure it's all going to be worth it.

It was a dreadful journey home on Friday night. I got home in the middle of the night. Chandni had gone to bed. Apparently she had made dinner for us, and it had spoiled.

I had tried to get a taxi to get me from the office to home, but there was a thunderstorm and no taxis were available. So I found a cycle and set off carrying three stacks of files which are immensely heavy when filled, and as I was out of practice, I had to stop several times on the way home. So I got home very tired and wet.

I apologized for waking Chandni, and told her about my troublesome journey.

'What happened to the car?' she asked anxiously.

'I've got rid of it,' I explained proudly. 'I've also got rid of the driver, all the fancy office furniture, and half my personal staff.'

'Government's been toppled!' she exclaimed.

'No.'

'Or you've been sacked!' she said. Chandni often jumps to the most ridiculous alarmist conclusions. I explained that it was

52

an economy drive and that I was setting an example of no frills, no luxuries and no privileges.

Chandni couldn't seem to understand. 'Hey Bhagvan!' she exploded. 'For twenty years as an opposition MP you have complained that you had no facilities and no help. Now you've been given them, and you're throwing them away.'

I tried to explain, but she wouldn't let me get a word in edgeways.

'For twenty years you've wanted to be a success—why did you want it if it brings no greater comfort than failure?'

I explained that this move would give me much greater power in the end.

Chandni was unimpressed. 'And how will you travel when you're Prime Minister? On a bullock-cart?'

Why can't she understand?

September 25th
Great progress today with the economy drive.

The office work is getting a bit behind, with twelve fewer people in my Private Office. Kaul is working overtime, and so am I, but clearly we didn't need all those people out there, reading my letters and writing my letters, making appointments and answering phone calls, drafting replies to questions and—basically—protecting me from the outside world. I don't need all these people to shield me. I am the people's representative. I should be available to one and all, shouldn't I?

However, we have to avoid screw-ups like this morning, when I arrived an hour and a half late to open a conference. What made it even more unfortunate was that it was the Time Management conference!

And, because we've abolished the night shift for cleaners (a really useful economy, in my view), I had a man in my office with a broom. Kaul and I had to keep moving around the room out of his way as we discussed the week's diary. But I'm sure these little wrinkles can be ironed out.

Tomorrow I have a vital meeting with Mr Shukla, Secretary, Ministry of Planning for the North-East Region, on the subject of staff reductions. I've never met him, but Kaul tells me he's eager to make cuts.

The biggest progress is in the media coverage I'm getting. A front-page story in the *Express*. Couldn't be better.

> ## No Luxury Lunches in Singh's New Austerity Regime
>
> 'Savings begin at home,' said Suryaprakash Singh today, as he ate a sandwich off a paper plate to set an example to India's pampered army of safari-suited bureaucrats.

Kaul Saheb recalls:

I remember Suryaprakash Singh's first economy drive only too well. I suspected, green though I still was, that Shri Rajnath Mathur had created a potentially disastrous situation.

It was impossible for me to run the Ministry Office single-handed, with just a couple of typists to help. Errors were bound to occur, and sooner or later there would be a calamity.

The calamity occurred sooner than I expected. On 26 September, the day after Suryaprakashji had received some favourable publicity, Saurav Dutta arrived at the Department without an appointment. Dutta was the President of the Administrative Service Transport Workers Union.

He demanded to see Mantriji at once, because of what he described as 'disturbing' rumours about cut-backs and redundancies affecting his members. The rumours were clearly generated by the numerous press stories of which Suryaprakash Singh was so ludicrously proud.

I told Dutta that nobody could see Mantriji without an appointment, and left the Private Office to go to the Speaker's Office. I was even having to run errands myself, as we were so short-staffed. Had we been fully staffed, Dutta would never even have got as far as Suryaprakashji's Private Office without an appointment. I left Ms Nagpal, the typist, to arrange an appointment for Dutta to see Mantriji.

Apparently, after I left the room, Shuklaji of the Ministry of Planning telephoned to say he had been called to the PMO [*The Prime Minister's Office —Ed.*], and could not keep his appointment. Dutta overheard, realized that Suryaprakashji was free at that moment, and walked straight into his office.

And because there were no other Private Secretaries, due to the economy drive, no one stopped him. And no one warned Mantriji that he was meeting Dutta instead of Shukla.

No greater mishap could have occurred.

September 26th
Today, everything collapsed in ruins. Total disaster.

I was expecting Mr Shukla of the Ministry of Planning (NE Region) at 3 p.m. A man walked into my office and naturally I assumed he was Shukla.

'Shuklaji?' I said.

'No,' he said, 'my name's Saurav Dutta. Mr Shukla has had

to cancel the meeting.'

Naturally, I assumed that Dutta had been sent by Shukla, and had come instead. So I interrupted, thanked him for coming and asked him to sit down and said, 'Look, Mr Dutta, before we start there's one point I have to emphasize. This simply must not get out. If the unions were to hear of this all hell would break loose.'

'I see,' he said.

'Of course there are going to be sacrifices,' I continued. 'You can't slim down a giant bureaucracy without getting rid of people. Ultimately, lots of people.'

He asked me if I wouldn't be holding discussions with the unions first.

I continued to dig my own grave. 'We'll go through the usual charade of consultation first,' I said, blithely unaware of the impending catastrophe, 'but you know what trades unionists are like. Just bloody-minded, self-serving and more intent on striking rather than working.' How could I have spoken like this to a total stranger?

'All of them?' he asked politely.

I was surprised by this question. I thought he should know; after all, he had to negotiate with them. 'Pretty much,' I said. 'All they're interested in is poaching members from each other or getting themselves on the TV—and they can never keep their big mouths shut.'

I remember quite clearly every word that I spoke. Each one is branded on my heart. Furthermore, it's all written down in front of me—in an interview Dutta gave to the *Express* as soon as he left my office.

Then the man asked me about drivers and transport service staff, specifically. 'They'll be the first to go,' I said. 'We're wasting a fortune on cars and drivers. And they're all useless fellows anyway.'

It was at this moment that Dutta revealed that he was not Mr Shukla's deputy, but was in fact the President of the Administrative Service Transport Workers Union. And he had come to my office to check our policy on the retirement scheme!

Oh my God!

September 28th

Yesterday and today there has been an acute shortage of Diwali cheer. [*Diwali this year was on October 3 —Ed.*]

All the Administrative Service drivers are on strike. I arrived yesterday morning, having read all about the strike in the press. All the papers quoted Saurav Dutta quoting me: 'Of course there's going to be job losses. Lots.'

I asked Kaul how he could have let this happen.

'AAHD, Mantriji,' he replied, unhappily.

I wasn't sure what he meant. 'AAHD?'

He explained, '*Akela Aadmi Hazaar Dikkatein.*' One person, a thousand problems—another idiotic civil service abbreviation. 'In normal circumstances . . .' he petered out. After all, we both knew how this tragedy had occurred.

Kaul reminded me of all my appointments for today. An office Diwali party, some meetings—nothing of any consequence. I spent the day dodging the press. I wanted to discuss the situation with Mathur, but apparently he was unavailable all day.

Chandni and I were invited to the French Ambassador's dinner party, at 8 p.m. I asked Kaul to get me my car—and then realized, as I spoke, that there were no drivers. I told him to call Chandni, to get her to bring our car in to pick me up.

Kaul had already thought of that, but apparently our car

had been giving trouble all day and Chandni wanted to take it to the garage. I got hold of her and told her the garage would wait—the car would get us from Shastri Bhavan to Chanakyapuri all right.

Chandni came to pick me up, and we set off.

Yet again I was wrong and the bloody car broke down halfway to Chanakyapuri. In the rush hour. In the pouring rain. I tried to fix it. I was wearing white, symbolic of my '*saadgi*' or 'simplicity' drive. I asked Chandni for the umbrella, she said I had it. I knew she had it. We shouted at each other, she got out and slammed her door, refused to go to a party looking like a Raj Kapoor heroine in a wet sari, and walked away. And I was left with the car blocking all of the rush hour traffic with horns blaring and drivers yelling abuse at me.

I got to the French Embassy an hour and a half late, soaked to the skin and covered in oil. I had three or four glasses of champagne right away—well, who wouldn't in the circumstances? I needed them!

When I left, not drunk exactly, but a bit the worse for wear, I must admit, I dropped my keys in the gutter beside the car. So I had to lie down to try and reach them, and some bastard from the press was there.

This morning I had a frightful hangover. I felt tired and sick. The press had really gone to town over my alleged drunkenness. They really are unbelievably irresponsible nowadays.

**Mr 'Simple Living, High Thinking'
Falls Down in Gutter After
Champagne Party**

Another paper's headline was SINGH TIRED AND EMOTIONAL AFTER EMBASSY RECEPTION. ['*Tired and emotional' being polite speak for 'had too much to drink' —Ed.*]

Mathur read it aloud, and remarked that it was slightly better, perhaps, than the first.

'Better?' I asked.

'Well . . . different, anyway,' said Mathur.

I asked if anyone had said anything beyond 'tired and emotional'. Kaul informed me that the Hindi papers said I had 'stumbled'. I didn't mind that quite so much, until Mathur added—for clarification—'*Kuch jyaada peeke ludak gaye,* actually.' ['*Drank too much and couldn't walk straight', to put it bluntly —Ed.*]

By now I felt that it could not get any worse. But I was wrong. Kaul produced today's lead story from the *Hindustan Times*, which, astonishingly and horrifyingly, claimed that I was recruiting extra staff to the MAA.

Suryaprakash Recruits 400 New Civil Servants

By Our Political Correspondent
In a so-called 'economy drive', Suryaprakash Singh, the Minister for Administrative Affairs, has recruited four hundred more civil servants.

I demanded an explanation from Mathur. And he had one ready, of course.

'Mantriji, you *asked* for these extra people. You demanded a complete study, a survey, facts and figures. These measures cannot be taken by non-people. If you create more work, more people have to be employed to do it. It's common sense.'

While I was taking this on the chin, he came in with another right hook to the head. 'And if you persist with your Special Bureaucratic Vigilance Committee, there'll be at least another four hundred new jobs there as well.'

I was shattered. My head was aching, I felt sick, my career seemed to be in ruins, I was being pilloried in the press and the only idea of mine that I had managed to push through since I had been here would now have to be abandoned.

Yet, throughout, from my first day here, all the permanent officials appear to have been doing their best to help me in every possible way. So are they completely inept? Or am I? Are they pretending to help while secretly obstructing my every move? Or are they incapable of understanding a new approach to the Department's work? Do they try to help me by pushing me towards the Ministry's policy? Is there a difference between the Minister's policy and the Ministry's policy? Why am I asking so many questions to which there is no known answer?

There was silence in the office. I didn't know what we were going to do about the four hundred new people supervising our economy drive or the four hundred new people for the Special Bureaucratic Vigilance Committee, or anything! I simply sat and waited and hoped that my head would stop thumping and that some idea would be suggested by someone sometime soon.

Mathur obliged. 'Mantriji . . . if we were to end the economy drive and close the Special Bureaucratic Vigilance Committee we could issue an immediate press announcement that you had axed eight hundred jobs.' He had obviously thought this out carefully in advance, for at this moment he produced a slim folder from under his arm. 'If you'd like to approve this draft . . .'

I couldn't believe the impertinence of the suggestion. Axed eight hundred jobs? 'But no one was ever doing these jobs,' I pointed out incredulously. 'No one's been appointed yet.'

'Even greater economy,' he replied instantly. 'We've saved eight hundred redundancy payments as well.'

'But . . .' I attempted to explain '. . . that's just phony. It's dishonest, it's juggling with figures, it's pulling the wool over people's eyes.'

'A government press release, in fact,' said Mathur. I've met some cynical politicians in my time, but this remark from my Secretary was a real eye-opener.

I nodded weakly. Clearly if I was to avoid the calamity of four hundred new people employed to make economies, I had to give up the four hundred new people in my cherished Vigilance Committee. A simple matter of give and take.

However, one vital central question, the question that was at the root of this whole debacle, remained completely unanswered. 'But Mathursaheb,' I said. 'How are we actually going to slim down the Administrative Service?'

There was a pause. Then he said: 'Well . . . I suppose we could get rid of one or two of the waiters, Mantriji.'

3

Nehle Pe Dahla
(Big Brother)

October 9th

Nothing of interest happened over Diwali. I spent the week in the constituency. I went to the usual Diwali parties for the constituency party, the old people's home, the general hospital, and assorted other gatherings, and it all went off quite well—I got my photo in the local newspaper four or five times, and avoided saying anything that committed me to anything.

I sensed a sort of resentment, though, and have become aware that I'm in a double-bind situation. The local party, the constituency, my family, all of them are proud of me for getting into the Cabinet—yet they are all resentful that I have less time to spend on them and are keen to remind me that I'm nothing special, just their local MP, and that I mustn't get 'too big for my boots'. They manage both to grovel and patronize me simultaneously. It's hard to know how to handle it.

If only I could tell them what life is really like in Parliament, they would know that there's absolutely no danger of my getting too big for my boots. Mathur will see to that.

Back to Delhi today for a TV interview on *Raaz Ki Baat*, with Ajay Kanchan. He asked me lots of awkward questions about the National Data Base.

We met in the Hospitality Room before the programme was recorded, and I tried to find out what angle he was taking. We were a little tense with each other, of course. [*Ajay Kanchan used to call the Hospitality Room the Hostility Room —Ed.*]

'We are going to talk about cutting government extravagance and that sort of thing, aren't we?' I asked, and immediately realized that I had phrased that rather badly.

Ajay Kanchan was amused. 'You want to talk about the government's extravagance?' he said with a twinkle in his eye.

'About the ways in which I'm cutting it down, I mean,' I said firmly.

'We'll get to that if we have time after the National Data Base,' he said.

I tried to persuade him that people weren't interested in the Data Base, that it was too trivial. He said he thought people were *very* interested in it, and were worried about Big Brother. This annoyed me, and I told Ajay he couldn't trivialize the National Data Base with that sort of sensationalistic approach. Ajay replied that as I had just said it was trivial already, so why not?

We left the Hospitality Room. In the studio, waiting for the programme to begin, a girl with a powder-puff kept flitting about and dabbing at my face and preventing me from thinking straight. She said I was getting a bit pink. 'We can't have that,' said Ajay jovially, 'what would the *Economic Times* say?'

Just before we started recording I remarked that I could well do without all those old questions like, 'Are we creating a Police State?'

In retrospect, perhaps this was a mistake.

[*We have found, in the NDTV News Archives, a complete transcript of Ajay Kanchan's interview with Suryaprakash Singh. It is printed overleaf* —Ed.]

THIS SCRIPT WAS TRANSCRIBED FROM AN ORIGINAL INTERVIEW, NOT COPIED FROM AN ORIGINAL SCRIPT. BECAUSE OF THE RISK OF MISHEARING AND THE DIFFICULTY IN SOME CASES OF IDENTIFYING INDIVIDUAL SPEAKERS, NDTV CANNOT VOUCH FOR ITS COMPLETE ACCURACY.

TOPIC: OCTOBER 9th INTERVIEW BETWEEN AJAY KANCHAN AND SHRI SURYAPRAKASH SINGH, MINISTER FOR ADMINISTRATIVE AFFAIRS

AJAY: Good evening. Is Big Brother watching you? To be more precise, did you know that the government is building up a dossier on you?

It's called by the harmless-sounding name of 'National Integrated Data Base'. What it means is that at the press of a button any civil servant can inspect just about every detail of your life—your tax, your medical record, the car you drive, the house you live in, motoring offences, periods of unemployment, children's school records, the lot—and that civil servant my happen to be your next door neighbour.

Recently there has been mounting concern over this powerful totalitarian weapon that the computer revolution has put in the government's hands. And the man who wields that weapon is the Minister for Administrative Affairs, Shri Suryaprakash Singh.

Mantriji, are you laying the foundations of a police state in this country?

SURYAPRAKASH: You know, I'm glad you asked me that question.

PAUSE

AJAY: In that case, Mantriji, could we have an answer?

SURYAPRAKASH: Yes, of course. I'm about to give you one, if I may. As I was saying, I'm glad you asked me that question. Because . . . well, because it's a question that a lot of people are asking. And why? Because . . . well, because a lot of people want to know the answer to it. And let's be quite clear about this—without beating about the bush—the plain fact of the matter is that it is a very important question indeed and people have a right to know.

PAUSE

AJAY: But Mantriji, you haven't given me an answer yet.

PAUSE

SURYAPRAKASH: I'm sorry, what was the question?

AJAY: How can I know that if I annoy you in this interview, you won't go back to your office, press a button and examine my tax returns, my hospital records, my police record . . .

SURYAPRAKASH: Oh, come on Ajayji, you know as well as I do that's not the way we do things in this country. Impossible to organize, anyway.

AJAY: Are you saying, Mantriji, that you would like to do those things, but you are too incompetent as yet?

SURYAPRAKASH: We're not incompetent. We could certainly check up on you if we wanted, that is, or, check up on *people*. Not *you*, of course, I don't mean you. But we're not interested in people. Er, that is, when I say we're not interested in people, I don't mean we're not *interested* in people, of course we are, I mean we're not interested in people *in that way*, if you know what I mean, in that we would never want to check up on . . . people.

AJAY: So what's the Data Base for, if it's not for checking up on people?

SURYAPRAKASH: You know, *that's* a very interesting question. (PAUSE) Look, the point is, people have just been alarmed by one or two silly press articles. It's a computer, that's all, it's for storing information and speeding up government business, thus avoiding a massive expansion of clerical staff.

Computers are good news.

AJAY: But if you put information into it, you're going to want information out of it!

SURYAPRAKASH: Not necessarily.

AJAY: So you're spending Rs 25 crores to store information you're never going to use?

SURYAPRAKASH: No—yes—no, well—yes, no, there will be safeguards.

AJAY: Such as?

SURYAPRAKASH: Well, we'll be looking at a whole range of possibilities. But it's a complex and highly technical business, you know.

AJAY: Well, perhaps I can help you. Let me read you an extract from an article written two years ago by the editor of *Manav Adhikar Patrika*. I think his name is Suryaprakash Singh. The article was called: 'Big Brother and the Not-so-Civil-Service'. I quote: 'if we are to protect the citizen from government spying, three measures are urgent. One, no civil servant must have access to another department's files without specific signed authorization from a Minister. Two, unauthorized snooping must be made a criminal offence. And three, every citizen should have the right to inspect his own personal file and get errors corrected.' What do you think of these proposals, Suryaprakashji? Alarmist?

SURYAPRAKASH: No, well, I stand by that, I mean, all these things must happen. Er, in due course.

AJAY: Why not now?

[Manav Adhikar Patrika *was a reformist paper which used to be edited by Suryaprakash. Manav Adhikar literally means Human Rights.—Ed.*]

SURYAPRAKASH: Well, the Taj Mahal wasn't built in a day. It's under review. But . . . well, these things take time you know.

AJAY: Suryaprakashji, am I talking to the former editor of *Manav Adhikar* or an Administrative Service spokesman?

SURYAPRAKASH: Well, we haven't talked yet about the safeguards. My new Bureaucratic Watch Dog Office, for instance, and . . .

AJAY: Suryaprakashji, it sounds as if we'll be needing a whole pack of watchdogs before very long. Thank you very much.

I thought I had waffled a bit, but Ajay told me I had stonewalled beautifully. We went back to Hospitality for a drink. I had water—two glasses, I needed it. I congratulated him on finding that old article of mine—a crafty move. He said that one of his research girls had found it, and asked if I wanted to meet her. I declined—and said I'd just go back to my office and have a look at her dossier!

I watched the programme in the evening. I think it was all right. I hope Mathur is pleased, anyway.

October 12th
There was divided opinion in the office this afternoon about my TV appearance three days ago. The matter came up at a 4 p.m. meeting with Mathur, Kaul and Dikshit.

Mathur and Kaul thought I had been splendid. Dignified and suitable. But Dikshit's voice was particularly notable by its silence, during this chorus of praise. When I asked him what he thought, he just snorted like a horse. I asked him to translate.

He didn't answer me, but turned to Mathur. 'I congratulate you,' he began, his manner even a little less charming than usual. 'Mantriji is now perfectly house-trained.' Mathur attempted to excuse himself and leave the room.

'If you'll excuse me, Dikshitji . . .'

Dikshit turned on me angrily. 'Do you realize you just say everything the Administrative Service programmes you to say? What are you, a man or a mouth?'

I started to excuse myself too, to get away from the subject.

Dikshit is actually beginning to get on my nerves. The chip on his shoulder about the Administrative Service is getting larger every day. I don't know why, because they have given him an office, he always has access to me, and they tell me that they

71

give him all possible papers that would be of use to him. Now he's started to take out his aggressions on me. He's like a bear with a sore head.

Mathur wanted to leave, and so did I. But Kaul started to give me my diary appointments—and that started another wrangle. Kaul told me I was to be in Ambala at 8 a.m. tomorrow, because I was to speak at the Conference of Fertilizer Dealers. Dikshit then reminded me that I was due in Sultanpur tomorrow night to address the by-election meeting. Kaul pointed out to me that I couldn't do both and I explained this to Dikshit. Dikshit pointed out that the by-election was important to us, whereas the Ambala trip was just an Administrative Service junket, and I explained this to Kaul. Kaul then reminded me that the conference had been in my diary for some time and that they all expected me to go to Ambala, and I explained this to Dikshit. Then Dikshit reminded me that the Party High Command expected me to go to Sultanpur, but I didn't explain this to Kaul because by this time I was tired of explaining and I said so. So Dikshit asked Kaul to explain why I was double booked, Kaul said no one had told him about Sultanpur, I asked Dikshit why he hadn't told Kaul, Dikshit asked me why I hadn't told Kaul, and I pointed out that I couldn't remember everything.

'I shall go to Ambala,' I said.

'Is that a decision, Mantriji?' asked Kaul.

'That's final,' I said.

Dikshit then played his trump card. 'The PM expects you to go to Sultanpur,' he said. Why hadn't he said this till now, stupid man? I asked if he was sure. He nodded.

'Kaul, I think I had better go to Sultanpur,' I said.

'Is that a decision?' asked Dikshit.

'Yes, that's final,' I said. 'And now I'm going home.'

'Is *that* a decision?' asked Mathur. I wasn't sure whether or not he was asking for clarification or making fun of me. I still find him completely baffling. Anyway, he continued, 'Mantriji, I think you've made the wrong decision, if I may say so. Your visit to Ambala is in the programme, it's been announced, you can't really get out of it.'

This was becoming impossible. They all seem to expect me to be in two places at once. I told them to find some way of getting me from Ambala to Sultanpur—train, car, helicopter, I didn't care how—and I would fulfil both engagements. 'And now,' I announced, 'I'm going home—that's final!'

'Finally final?' asked Kaul.

His intentions are equally obscure. As I left, Kaul gave me two files and asked me to be sure to do them tonight because of all the Committee papers for tomorrow and letters that have to go off before the weekend.

'And if you don't do your homework,' said Dikshit in a rather poor imitation of Kaul, 'your teacher will punish you.'

I really don't have to put up with all this aggravation from Dikshit. I'm stuck with these damn permanent officials, but Dikshit is only there at my express invitation. I may have to remind him of this, very soon.

When I got home Chandni was packing. 'Leaving me at last?' I enquired jovially. She reminded me that it was our anniversary tomorrow and we had arranged to go to Mussoorie.

I was appalled! I tried to explain to her about the trips to Ambala and Sultanpur. She said that she didn't want to spend her anniversary in Ambala and Sultanpur, particularly not at a Conference for Fertilizer Dealers. I could see her point. She told me to cancel my meetings, I said I couldn't, so she said she'd go to Mussoorie without me.

So I phoned Kaul. I told him it was my wife's wedding anniversary—Chandni said, 'Yours too'—and mine too. Kaul made some silly joke about a happy coincidence. I told him I was going to Mussoorie tomorrow, instead, and that it was final and that I knew I had said it was final before but now this was really final—I told him he'd have to sort everything out. Then he talked for three minutes and when I rang off I was still going to Ambala and Sultanpur tomorrow.

These civil servants can talk you in or out of anything. I just don't seem to know my own mind any more.

Chandni and I fumed in silence for a while, and finally I asked her the really important question of the day: had she seen me on my TV interview?

'I saw someone who looked like you.'

I asked her what that was supposed to mean. She didn't answer.

'Dikshit said that I'm just an Administrative Service mouthpiece,' I muttered resentfully.

Chandni said, 'Yes.'

I was shocked. 'You mean . . . you agree?'

'Of course,' she said. 'You could have hired an actor to say it all for you. He'd have said it better. And while you're at it, why not just sign your letters with a rubber stamp or get a Deputy Secretary to sign them—they write them anyway.'

I tried to remain dignified. 'Deputy Secretaries do not write my letters,' I said. 'Under-Secretaries write them.'

'I rest my case, my Lord,' she said.

'You think I've become a puppet too?'

'I do. Don't you?'

I must say I was feeling pretty hurt and defeated. I sighed and sat on the bed. I honestly felt near to tears. Is this how a

Cabinet Minister usually feels, I wondered, or am I just an utter failure? I couldn't see what was wrong, but something certainly was.

'I don't know what to do about it,' I said quietly. 'I'm just swamped by the volume of work. I'm so depressed.'

Chandni suggested that, as we weren't going to Mussoorie after all, we might at least go for dinner to a Chinese restaurant. I told her that I couldn't, because Kaul had told me to work through some files tonight.

Chandni then said something which changed my whole perception of the situation. She said, 'What do you mean, "Kaul told me"? When you edited *Manav Adhikar* you were quite different—you went in, you told people what to do, demanded what you wanted, and you got it! What's changed? You're the same man—you're just allowing them to walk all over you.'

And suddenly, I saw that it was true. She was right. That was why Dikshit had been getting at me too. Either I get them by the throat or they'll get me by the throat! It's the law of the jungle, just like in the Cabinet.

'How many articles did you reject and tear up in those days?' she asked.

'At least twenty every day,' I remembered.

'And how many official papers have you torn up?'

'None,' I told her. 'I'm not allowed to.'

She smiled reproachfully at me, and I realized that I still hadn't broken out of this destructive pattern of behaviour.

'Not allowed to?' She held my hand. 'But you are the Mantri. You can do anything you like.' She's right. I am. I can. And, somehow, all my officials have house-trained me. I see it now. Honestly, I'm so grateful to Chandni, she has such remarkable common sense. Well, they're going to get quite a surprise.

Suddenly, I can't wait to get to the office. My new resolution is: Take Charge.

October 16th
Today was better.

But only a little better. My attitude was fine, but unfortunately theirs didn't seem to change all that much.

I summoned Mathur to my office. I don't think he liked being summoned. Then I told him that Dikshit was absolutely correct, and Ajay Kanchan too—the National Data Base has to be organized differently.

To my surprise, he agreed meekly.

'Ji Mantriji,' he murmured.

'We are going to have all possible built-in safeguards,' I went on.

'Ji Mantriji,' he murmured again.

'Right away,' I added.

This took him by surprise. 'Er . . . what precisely do you mean, Mantriji, right away?'

'I mean right away,' I said.

'Oh I see, you mean *right away*, Mantriji.'

'Yes, Mathursaheb.'

So far, so good. But, having totally accepted at the start of the conversation that it was all to be different, he now started to chip away at my resolve.

'The only thing is,' he began, 'perhaps I should remind you that we are still in the early months of this government and there's an awful lot to get on with, Mantriji . . .'

I interrupted. 'Mathursaheb,' I reiterated firmly, 'we are changing the rules of the Data Base. Now!'

'But you can't, Mantriji,' he said, coming out into the open.

76

'I can,' I said, remembering my stern talk from Chandni last night. 'I'm the Mantri.'

He changed tactics again. 'Indeed you are, Mantriji,' he said, rapidly switching from bullying to grovelling, 'and quite an excellent Mantriji at that, if I may say so.'

I brushed this aside. 'Never mind the soft soap, Mathursaheb,' I replied. 'I want all citizens to have the right to check their own file, and I want legislation to make unauthorized access to personal files illegal.'

'Very well,' said Mathur. 'It shall be done.'

This rather took the wind out of my sails. 'Right,' I said. 'Good. Then we go ahead.' I wondered what the catch was.

I was right. There was a catch. Mathur took this opportunity to explain to me that we can go ahead, if the Cabinet agrees, and take the matter to the Law Ministry and the Ministerial Committee, and then we can go ahead to the Official Committee. After that, of course, it's all plain sailing—straight to the Cabinet Committee! And then back to the Cabinet itself. I interrupted to point out that we had *started* with the Cabinet.

'Only the policy, Mantriji,' explained Mathur. 'At this juncture the Cabinet will have to consider the specific proposals.'

I conceded the point, but remarked that after going back to the Cabinet we could then go ahead. Mathur agreed—but with the proviso that if the Cabinet raised any questions, which it almost certainly would, the proposals would then have to go back to the Law Ministry, the Ministerial Committee, the Official Committee, the Cabinet Committee and the Cabinet again.

'I know all this,' I said brusquely. 'I'm assuming that Cabinet will raise no objections.' Mathur raised his eyebrows and visibly refrained from comment.

I didn't know all this at all, actually—the complex mechanics of passing legislation don't ever really become clear to you when you're in the Opposition or on the back benches.

'So after the Cabinet, we go ahead. Right?'

'Yes,' he said, 'to the Leader of the House Committee. And then to Parliament—where there's the Committee stage of course.'

But suddenly the penny dropped. Suddenly I realized he was blurring the whole issue. A blindfold dropped away from my eyes, as if by magic. 'Mathursaheb,' I said, 'you're talking about legislation—but I'm talking about administrative and procedural changes.'

Mathur smiled complacently. 'If members of the public are to have the right to take legal action, then legislation is necessary and it will be very complicated.'

I had the answer to that. 'Legislation is not necessary in order for the citizen to be able to see his own file, is it?'

Mathur thought carefully about this. 'No-o-o-o,' he finally said, with great reluctance.

'Then we'll go ahead with that,' I said. Round one to me, I thought.

But Mathur had not yet conceded even that much. 'Mantriji,' he began, 'we could manage that slightly quicker, but there are an awful lot of administrative problems as well.'

'Look,' I said, 'this must have come up before. This Data Base has been in preparation for years, it hasn't just materialized overnight—these problems must have been discussed.'

'Yes indeed,' he agreed.

'So what conclusions have been reached?' I asked.

Mathur didn't reply. At first I thought he was thinking. Then I thought he hadn't heard me, for some curious reason. So I asked him again, 'What conclusions have been reached?' a little louder, just in case. Again there was no visible reaction. I thought he had become ill.

'Mathursaheb,' I asked, becoming a little concerned for his health and sanity, 'can you hear me?'

'My lips are sealed,' he replied, through unsealed lips. I asked him what exactly he meant.

'I am not at liberty to discuss the previous government's plans,' he said. I was baffled.

'Why not?' I asked.

'Mantriji—would you like everything that you have said and done in the privacy of this office to be revealed subsequently to one of your opponents?'

I had never thought of that. Of course, I'd be absolutely horrified. It would be a constant threat. I would never be able to speak freely in my own office.

Mathur knew that he had scored a bull's-eye. He pressed home his advantage. 'We cannot give your political opponents ammunition against you—nor vice versa.'

Of course, I could see his point but there was one essential difference in this instance. I pointed out to Mathur that Sushilji was my predecessor, and he wouldn't mind. He's a very decent chap. After all, the Data Base is not a party political matter, politicians of all parties are united on this.

But Mathur wouldn't budge. 'It's the principle, Mantriji,' he said.

So I suppose I'll never know what went on before I came here. I can't see a way around that.

So where have we got to? We've established that we don't need legislation to enable the citizen to see his own file, but that there are numerous unspecified admin. problems that have to be solved first.

One other thing occurred today. Kaul said that because of

79

the adverse (Kaul called it 'not entirely favourable') press reaction to my appearance on *Raaz Ki Baat*, Channel 2 wants me to appear on their programme *India in Focus*. Funny how television is never interested when you've got an important announcement to make, but the moment some trivial thing goes wrong the phone never stops ringing. At first I told him to decline, but he said that if I don't appear they'll do the item anyway, and no one will be there to state my case.

I asked Mathur what I was to say about safeguards for the Data Base, in view of our very limited progress today. 'Perhaps you could remind them, Mantriji, that the Taj Mahal wasn't built in a day,' he said.

Big help! As I review the meeting, writing it all down for this diary, I now feel that I got absolutely nowhere today. But there must be some way to get Mathur and the MAA to do what I tell them.

October 17th
Today, by a lucky chance, I learned a bit more about dealing with Mathur.

I bumped into Sushilji, coming out of Parliament. I asked if I could join him, and he was only too pleased.

'How are you enjoying being in the Opposition?' I asked him jocularly. Like the good politician he is, he didn't exactly answer my question. 'How are you enjoying being in government?' he replied.

I could see no reason to beat about the bush, and I told him that, quite honestly, I'm not enjoying it as much as I had expected to.

'Mathursaheb's got you under control?' he smiled.

I dodged that one, but said that it's so very hard to get

anything done. He nodded, so I asked him, 'Did you get anything done?'

'Almost nothing,' he replied cheerfully. 'But I didn't catch on to his technique till I had been there for nearly two years— and then of course there was the election.'

It emerged from the conversation that the technique in question was Mathur's system for stalling.

According to Sushilji, it's in five stages. I made a note during our conversation, for future reference.

Stage One: Mathur will say that the administration is in its early months and there's an awful lot of other things to get on with. (Sushilji clearly knows his stuff. That is just what Mathur said to me yesterday.)

Stage Two: If I persist past Stage One, he'll say that he quite appreciates the intention, something certainly ought to be done— but is this the right way to achieve it?

Stage Three: If I'm still undeterred he will shift his ground from how I do it to when I do it, i.e. 'Mantriji, this is not the time, for all sorts of reasons.'

Stage Four: Lots of ministers settle for Stage Three according to Sushilji. But if not, Mathur will then say that the policy has run into difficulties—technical, political and/or legal. (Legal difficulties are best because they can be made totally incomprehensible and can go on for ever.)

Stage Five: Finally, because the first four stages have taken up to three years, the last stage is to say that 'we're getting rather near to the run-up to the next general election—so we can't be sure of getting the policy through'.

The stages can be made to last three years because at each stage Mathur will do absolutely nothing until the Minister chases him. And he assumes, rightly, that the Minister has too much

81

else to do. [*The whole process is called Creative Inertia —Ed.*]

Sushilji asked me what the policy was that I was trying to push through. When I told him that I was trying to make the National Integrated Data Base less of a Big Brother, he roared with laughter.

'I suppose he's pretending it's all new?'

I nodded.

'Clever old fellow,' said Sushilji. 'We spent years on that. We almost had a White Paper ready to bring out, but the election was called. I've done it all.'

I could hardly believe my ears. I asked about the administrative problems. Sushilji said there were none—all solved. And Sushilji guessed that my enquiries about the past were met with silence—'clever devil, he's wiped the slate clean'.

Anyway, now I know the five stages, I should be able to deal with Mathur quite differently. Sushilji advised me not to let on that we had had this conversation, because it would spoil the fun. He also warned me of the 'Three Varieties of Civil Service Silence', which would be Mathur's last resort if completely cornered:

1 The silence when they do not want to tell you the facts: *Discreet Silence*.

2 The silence when they do not intend to take any action: *Stubborn Silence*.

3 The silence when you catch them out and they haven't a leg to stand on—they imply that they could vindicate themselves completely if only they were free to tell all, but they are too honourable to do so: *Courageous Silence*.

Finally Sushilji told me what Mathur's next move would be. He asked how many files they had given me for tonight: 'Three? Four?'

'Five,' I admitted, somewhat shamefaced.

'Five?' He couldn't hide his astonishment at how badly I was doing. 'Have they told you that you needn't worry too much about the fifth?'

I nodded.

'Right. Well, I'll bet you that at the bottom of the fifth file will be a submission explaining why any new moves on the Data Base must be delayed—and if you never find it or read it they'll do nothing further, and in six months' time they'll say they told you all about it.'

There was one more thing I wanted to ask Sushilji, who really had been extremely kind and helpful. He's been in office for years, in various government posts. So I said to him, 'Look Sushilji, you know all the Administrative Service tricks.'

'Not all,' he grinned, 'just a few hundred.'

'Right,' I said. 'Now how do you defeat them? How do you make them do something they do not want to do?'

Sushilji smiled ruefully, and shook his head. 'My dear fellow,' he replied, 'if I knew that I wouldn't be in the Opposition.'

October 18th

I did my boxes till so late last night that I'm writing up yesterday's discoveries a day late.

Sushilji had been most helpful to me. When I got home I told Chandni all about it over dinner. She couldn't understand why Sushilji, as a member of the Opposition, would have been so helpful.

I explained to her that the Opposition aren't really the opposition. They're just called the Opposition. But, in fact, they are the opposition in exile. The Administrative Service is the opposition in residence.

Then after dinner I did the files and sure enough, at the bottom of the fifth file, I found a submission on the Data Base. Not merely at the bottom of the fifth box—to be doubly certain the submission had somehow slipped into the middle of an eighty-page report on Welfare Procedures.

By the way, Sushilji had also lent me all his private papers on the Data Base, which he kept when he left office. Very useful!

The submission contained the expected delaying phrases: 'Subject still under discussion . . . programme not finalized . . . nothing precipitate . . . failing instructions to the contrary propose await developments.'

Chandni suggested that I ring Mathur and tell him that I disagree. I was reluctant—it was past 2 a.m., and he'd be fast asleep.

'Why should he sleep while you're working?' Chandni asked me. 'After all, he's had you on the run for weeks. Now it's your turn.'

'I couldn't possibly do that,' I said.

Chandni looked at me. 'What's his number?' I asked, as I reached for our address book.

Chandni added reasonably, 'After all, if it was in the fifth file you couldn't have found it any earlier, could you?'

Mathur answered the phone with a curious sort of grunting noise. I had obviously woken him up. 'Sorry to ring you so late, you weren't in the middle of dinner, were you?'

'No,' he said, sounding somewhat confused, 'we had dinner some while ago, Mantriji. What's the time?'

I told him it was 2.05 a.m.

'Good God!' He sounded as though he had really woken up now. 'What's the crisis?'

'No crisis. I'm still going through my files and I knew you'd still be hard at it.'

'Oh yes,' he said, stifling a yawn. 'Nose to the grindstone.'
I told him I had just got to the paper on the Data Base.

'Oh, you've found . . .' he corrected himself without pausing,
'you've read it.'

I told him that I thought he needed to know, straight away,
that I wasn't happy with it, that I knew he'd be grateful to have
a little extra time to work on something else, and that I hoped he
didn't mind my calling him.

'Always a pleasure to hear from you, Mantriji,' he said, and
I think he slammed down the phone.

After I rang off I realized I had forgotten to tell him to come
and talk about it before Cabinet tomorrow. I was about to pick
up the phone when Chandni said, 'Don't ring him now.'

I was surprised by this sudden show of kindness and
consideration for Mathur, but I agreed. 'No, perhaps it is a bit
late.'

She smiled. 'Yes. Just give him another ten minutes.'

October 19th
This morning I made a little more progress in my battle for
control over Mathur and my Department, though the battle is
not yet won.

But I had with me my notes from the meeting with Sushilji,
and—exactly as Sushilji had predicted—Mathur put his stalling
technique into practice.

'Mathursaheb,' I began, 'have you drafted the proposed
safeguards for the Data Base?'

'Mantriji,' he replied plausibly, 'I quite appreciate your
intention and I fully agree that there is a need for safeguards but
I'm wondering if this is the right way to achieve it.'

'It's my way,' I said decisively, and I ticked off the first objection in my little notebook. 'And that's my decision.'

Mathur was surprised that his objection had been brushed aside so early, without protracted discussion—so surprised that he went straight on to his second stage.

'Even so Mantriji,' he said, 'this is not really the time, for all sorts of reasons.'

I ticked off number two in my notebook, and replied, 'It is the perfect time—safeguards have to develop parallel with systems, not after them—that's common sense.'

Mathur was forced to move on to his third objection. Sushilji really has analysed his technique well.

'Unfortunately, Mantriji,' he said doggedly, 'we have tried this before, but, well . . . we have run into all sorts of difficulties.'

I ticked off number three in my little book. Mathur had noticed this by now, and tried to look over my shoulder to see what was written there. I held the book away from him.

'What sort of difficulties?' I enquired.

'Technical, for example,' said Mathur.

Thanks to a careful study of Sushilji's private papers, I had the answer ready. 'No problem at all,' I said airily. 'I've been doing some research. We can use the CBI dossier software and also the Voter Identity Card kit. No technical problems.'

Mathur was getting visibly rattled, but he persisted. 'There are also formidable administrative problems. All departments are affected. An interdepartmental committee will have to be set up . . .'

I interrupted him in mid-sentence. 'No,' I said firmly. 'I think you'll find, if you look into it, that the existing security procedures are adequate. This can just be an extension. Anything else?'

Mathur was gazing at me with astonishment. He just couldn't

work out how I was so thoroughly in command of the situation. Was I just making a series of inspired guesses, he wondered. As he didn't speak for a moment, I decided to help him out.

'Legal problems?' I suggested helpfully.

'Ji Mantriji,' he agreed at once, hoping that he had me cornered at last. Legal problems were always his best bet.

'Good, good,' I said, and ticked off the last but one stage on my little list. Again he tried to see what I had written down.

'There is a question,' he began carefully, 'of whether we have the legal power . . .'

'I'll answer it,' I announced grandly. 'We do.' He was looking at me in wonderment. 'All personnel affected are bound by their staff service agreement anyway.'

He couldn't argue because, of course, I was right. Grasping at straws he said, 'But Mantriji, there will have to be extra staffing—are you sure you will get it through Cabinet and the Parliamentary Party?'

'Quite sure,' I said. 'Anything else?' I looked at my list. 'No, nothing else. Right, so we go ahead?'

Mathur was silent. I wondered whether he was being discreet, stubborn or courageous. Stubborn, I think.

Eventually, I spoke. 'You're very silent,' I remarked. There was more silence. 'Why are you so silent, by the way?'

He realized that he had to speak, or the game was up. 'Mantriji, you do not seem to realize how much work is involved.'

Casually, I enquired if he had never investigated safeguards before, under another government perhaps, as I thought I remembered written answers to Parliamentary questions in the past.

His reply went rather as follows: 'Mantriji, in the first place, we've agreed that the question is not fair. In the second place, if there had been investigations, which there haven't or not necessarily, or I am not at liberty to say if there have, there would have been a project team which, had it existed, on which I cannot comment, would now be disbanded if it had existed and the members returned to their original departments, had there indeed been any such members.' Or words to that effect.

I waited till the torrent of useless language came to a halt, and then I delivered my ultimatum. I told him that I wanted safeguards on the use of the Data Base made available immediately. He told me it wasn't possible. I told him it was. He told me it wasn't. I told him it was. We went on like that like a couple of three-year-olds, glowering at each other, till Kaul popped in.

I didn't want to reveal that Sushilji had told me of the safeguards that were ready and waiting, because then I'd have no more aces up my sleeve.

While I contemplated this knotty problem, Kaul reminded me of my engagements: Cabinet committee meeting at ten, then the Anglo-Indian Society lunch, and the *India in Focus* interview this evening. I asked him if he could get me out of the TV interview. 'Not really, Mantriji,' he answered, 'it's been announced on TV. There's nothing that can be done now.'

And suddenly I saw the light. The most wonderful plan formed in my mind.

I told Mathur and Kaul to be sure to watch me on TV tonight.

[*The transcript of Suryaprakash Singh's appearance that night on* India in Focus *follows. It contains his first truly memorable victory over his officials —Ed.*]

THIS IS AN UNCORRECTED TRANSCRIPT ONLY. NOT FOR
CIRCULATION WITHOUT PROGRAMME CONTROLLER'S
APPROVAL.

INDIA IN FOCUS—October 19th—SURYAPRAKASH SINGH INTERVIEW

SUNIL BATRA: And our man on the spot tonight is the Minister of
Administrative Affairs, Shri Suryaprakash Singh, the man at the
heart of the Big Brother computer controversy.

Mantriji, as you know there's been an outcry this week about the
dossier that the Administrative Service Bureaucracy is apparently
starting to build up on every citizen in the country. It is rumoured
that this is not your own policy, that you wish to have safeguards
for the individual citizen, but that you are being totally frustrated
every step of the way by the Administrative Service machine.

SURYAPRAKASH SINGH: You know Batrasaheb, there's a lot of
nonsense talked about the Administrative Service. It is actually a
marvellous, efficient, professional organization capable of
tremendous effort end speed. It is full of talented, dedicated people
who do all they can to help government policies become law.

SUNIL BATRA: Thank you for the commercial, Mantriji. If we
could start the programme now?

SURYAPRAKASH SINGH: The fact is, the Administrative Service
and I are in complete accord on this whole matter, and our proposals
are now ready for publication.

I am happy to announce tonight that, within one month, every
citizen of India will have the absolute right to inspect his or her
personal file and to check any information that he or she has ever
supplied to the government.

Secondly, no civil servant will be allowed to examine personal
files from another Department without written authority from a
Minister. And I shall be announcing, in Parliament next week,

legislation enabling the citizens to take legal action against any civil servant who gains unauthorized access to his file.

SUNIL BATRA: Well . . . that's, er . . . well, that's very interesting end encouraging, Mantriji. Why did you not say so earlier and put people's minds at rest?

SURYAPRAKASH SINGH: Frankly, Sunilji, I didn't believe the Administrative Service could meet these deadlines. But they've convinced me that they can. Indeed my Secretary is staking his reputation on it.

  And, if not, heads will roll.

Kaul Saheb recalls:
Suryaprakash Singh always gave me the credit for this brilliant ploy, because of the unintentional double meaning of my remark, 'it's been announced, there's nothing that can be done now'.

I well remember that Mathursaheb's face was a picture when Suryaprakashji made his statement—especially at the moment when he said that his Secretary had staked his reputation on it.

He turned to me and said, 'It can't be done.' I made no reply.

Then he said to me, 'Well Kaul, what do you make of Mantriji's performance?'

I was obliged to say that, in my opinion, it was checkmate.

October 20
Today was my happiest day since I became a Minister.

'Did you see me on the TV last night?' I asked Mathur cheerfully as he came into the office looking like someone at a funeral.

'Of course,' he replied, tight-lipped.

Actually, it didn't matter whether he had seen me or not, because my TV appearance was completely reported in the morning press.

'How was I?' I asked innocently. 'Good?'

'A most remarkable performance, Mantriji, if I may say so,' he answered with studied ambiguity.

'You may, you may,' I said, affecting not to notice it.

'Mantriji, we have been working very hard all night, and I'm happy to be able to inform you that we have come up with some draft proposals that would enable you to achieve your desired objectives by the stated dates.'

In other words, he had spent five minutes digging out from

the files the proposals agreed last year when Sushilji was Minister.

'Well done, Mathursaheb,' I said ingenuously. 'You see, I told the nation how splendid you are and I was right. I had every confidence in you.'

'Quite so, Mantriji,' he said through clenched teeth.

He got out a folder containing his proposals.

'Are those your proposals?' I asked.

'Yes.'

'Here are mine,' I said, and produced a folder too.

'You have proposals too?' He was surprised.

I told Mathur to read his proposed safeguards. Then I would read mine. And we would see how they compared.

Mahtur started reading. 'One—Personal Data. 1A. Safeguards must be applied with reference to . . .'

I could resist it no longer. Reading from my folder, I joined in, and together, in unison, we read: '. . . Two criteria—the need to know and the right to know. 1A(i). The need to know. Only those officials for whom the information was submitted may be deemed, prima facie, to have a need to know.'

We looked at each other.

'We seem to be of the same mind,' I remarked.

'Where did those proposals come from, Mantriji?' he demanded. I said nothing. After a few moments he repeated, 'Where did those proposals come from?'

'Mathursaheb,' I replied in a tone of slight reproof, 'my lips are sealed.'

4

The Hit List

October 22nd

It has become clear to me, as I sit here for my usual Sunday evening period of contemplation and reflection, that my driver knows a great deal more than I realized about what is going on in South Block.

South Block is the most secretive place in the world. The great emphasis on avoidance of error (which is what the Administrative Service is really about, since that is their only real incentive) also means that avoidance of publication is equally necessary.

As Ramansaheb [*Shri Vijay Raman, the Cabinet Secretary — Ed.*] is reported to have said some months ago, 'If no one knows what you're doing, then no one knows what you're doing wrong.'

[*Perhaps this explains why government forms are always so hard to understand. Forms are written to protect the person who is in charge of the form.—Ed.*]

And so the way information is provided—or withheld—is the key to running the government smoothly.

This concern with the avoidance of error leads to the need to commit everything to paper—civil servants copy everything, and send copies to all their colleagues. (This is also because 'chaps don't like to leave other chaps out', as Kaul once explained to me.) The Finance Ministry was rather more competent before the invention of xerox than it is now, because its officials had so much less to read (and therefore less to confuse them).

The civil servants' hunger for paper is insatiable. They want all possible information sent to them, and they send all possible information to their colleagues. It amazes me that they find the time to do anything other than catch up with other people's paperwork. If indeed they do.

It is also astonishing that so little of this vast mass of

typescript ever becomes public knowledge—a very real tribute to South Block's talent for secrecy. For it is axiomatic with civil servants that information should only be revealed to their political 'masters' when absolutely necessary, and to the public when absolutely unavoidable.

But I now see that I can learn some useful lessons from their methods. For a start, I must pay more attention to Kaul and my driver. I resolve today that I will not let false pride come between the driver and me—in other words, I shall no longer pretend that I know more than my driver does. Tomorrow, when he picks me up, I shall ask him to tell me anything that he has picked up, and I shall tell him that he mustn't assume that ministers know more secrets than drivers.

On second thoughts, I don't need to tell him that—he knows already!

As for the Private Secretaries' grapevine, it was most interesting to learn last week that Mathur had had a telling-off from Shri Vijay Raman, the Cabinet Secretary. This will have profoundly upset Mathur, who above all values the opinions of his colleagues.

For there is one grapevine with even more knowledge and influence than the Private Secretaries' or the drivers'—and that is the Secretaries' grapevine. (Cabinet colleagues, of course, have a hopeless grapevine because they are not personal friends, don't know each other all that well, and hardly ever see each other except in Cabinet or in the corridors.)

This telling-off could also, I gather, affect his chances of becoming Secretary to the Cabinet on Raman's retirement, or screw up the possibility of his finding a comfortable job overseas.

Happily, this is not my problem—and when I mentioned it to my spies, both Kaul and the driver agreed (independently) that Mathur would not be left destitute. Apart from his massive index-linked pension, a former Secretary is always fixed up with a job if he wants it—fisheries or *pashupalan* [*animal husbandry —Ed.*], or something.

As for Kaul, I have recently been impressed with his loyalty to me. He seems to be giving me all the help he possibly can without putting his own career at risk. In fact, I am almost becoming concerned about the amount of rapport, decency and goodwill that exist between us—if he exhibits a great deal more of these qualities he will almost certainly be moved elsewhere. There may come a time when the Department feels that the more use he is to me the less use he is to them.

October 23rd
I was sitting at my desk this afternoon going through some letters when Kaul came in holding something behind his back.

'Excuse me, Mantriji,' he said. 'There's something in the press about you that I think you ought to see.'

I was pleased. 'About me? That's nice.'

Kaul looked bleak. 'Well . . .' he swallowed, 'I'm afraid it's in *Sansani Khoj*.'

Trembling, I took the offending rag and held it away from me with my forefinger and thumb. I didn't have the courage to open it. Normally the press officer brings you your own press cuttings. If he had given his job to Kaul, it meant terrible news. No prizes for guessing which, in the case of *Sansani Khoj*.

'They're . . . um . . . exposing something,' said Kaul.

Panic thoughts flashed through my mind. In that instant my whole life passed before me. Was it that HFDC Consultancy, I wondered. Or that character reference I wrote for Dr Chopra? Or that wretched party at Captain Sharma's?

I didn't even dare mention these to Kaul. So I put a good face on it. 'Well,' I said, chin up, 'what have they made up about me to put in their *raddi-chaap* little newspaper?' [*Raddi-chaap is Hindi for squalid, or, rubbish —Ed.*]

'Perhaps you had better read it yourself,' he said. So I did. It was acutely embarrassing.

पिछले हफ्ते हमने सरकार द्वारा कराई गई खुफिया निगरानी का जिक्र किया था। हमारे पास जो दस्तावेज हैं वे साबित करते हैं कि वर्तमान सरकार के एक मंत्री जब विपक्ष के नेता थे तो उनके फ़ोन टैप किए जाते थे और उनके ऊपर चौबीसों घंटे निगरानी रखी जा रही थी। वे और कोई नहीं आज के अप्रतिहत सूर्यप्रकाश हैं।
और अब सूर्यप्रकाश का मंत्रालय ही सारे डिपार्टमैंट्स को टैपिंग एक्विपमैंट सप्लाइ कर रहा है। सूर्यप्रकाश को इस सरकार का सेंध मार कहा जाय तो ग़लत नहीं होगा।

[*Here is a rough translation of the piece for our readers:*
Last week the Khoj *exposed before its readers the scandal of the government's security practices. New documents that have come into our possession reveal that a member of the present Cabinet was subjected to phone-tapping, bugging and twenty-four-hour surveillance while in the Opposition. The Minister in question is none other than the one-and-only Suryaprakash Singh, whose Ministry of Administrative Affairs is now responsible for supplying*

all the government's computerized bugging equipment.
Presumably this makes him the government's chief
bugger.—Ed.]

I sent for Mathur at once. I had to establish whether or not
this lie was true.

One aspect of this squalid little story puzzled me in particular.
'What does that mean—"*apratihat*"?' I asked Kaul.

'I think it means "unstoppable", Mantriji,' he explained.

That's okay, if that's what it means, but it seems a little too
generous for *Sansani Khoj*. I must remember to look it up
sometime.

Mathur arrived, was shown the piece, and actually had the
audacity to laugh at the bugger joke.

'Is this true?' I demanded.

'Oh absolutely not, Mantriji,' he replied firmly. I was relieved
for a moment, until he went on, 'It's only one of their little jokes.
I don't think that anyone actually supposes that you are a
bu . . . I mean . . . that is . . ,'

I exploded. 'Mathursaheb, I'm not talking about that
nonsensical little joke. I'm asking you if the gist of this story is
true—was I once under surveillance and am I now responsible
for the bugging equipment?'

'Surely . . .' said Mathur evasively, and how well I recognize
the tactics by now! 'Surely you don't believe what you read in
that *raddi-chaap* little newspaper?' ['*Raddi-chaap little*
newspaper' was clearly South Block general slang usage for
Sansani Khoj *at this time —Ed.*]

I asked him again. Was it accurate?

Mathur again declined to give a straight answer. 'I don't
think we should take it too seriously, Mantriji,' he replied suavely.

I saw red. I told him that I regard this as an outrageous and intolerable intrusion into my privacy. If he didn't see anything wrong with it, I certainly did. And I propose to take it very seriously indeed. I reminded Mathur that the article stated that I, a free citizen, and furthermore an MP, have been under total surveillance. Surveillance is an attack on democracy. I asked Mathur if he was aware that it contravenes the Constitution of India.

He remained calm. 'Surveillance,' he said, 'is an indispensable weapon in the battle against organized crime.'

I was incredulous. That's no reason for bugging me, a politician.

'Mathursaheb,' I asked, 'are you describing politicians as practitioners of organized crime?'

He smiled. 'Well . . . disorganized crime too,' he joked. I was not amused. He realized that he was going too far, and hastily started to repair the damage. 'No, seriously, Mantriji . . .'

I cut him short. I reminded him of my own track record, one that made this situation particularly awkward for me.

'While I was editor of *Manav Adhikar* I wrote an editorial criticizing this kind of intrusion. Furthermore, I started a nationwide petition against bureaucratic fellows snooping and phone-tapping. And *now* I learn,' I continued angrily, 'from *Sansani Khoj*, please note, and not from you—that *I*, of *all* people, am in charge of the whole technical side of it.' It was all profoundly embarrassing.

Mathur merely nodded.

I asked the inevitable question.

'Why didn't you tell me about this?'

'Because,' came the inevitable answer, 'you didn't ask.'

'Well,' I said, 'thank God for the free press. Thank God for at least one brave, open and fearless journal in this country.'

Kaul started to remind me that I had previously described it differently, but I stopped him. However, I took the opportunity to explain to him that he really must sharpen up his political antennae. He needs to learn to adjust more flexibly to a developing situation.

He took my point, I think—I hope!

The next question inevitably raised by these revelations concerned the tapes and/or transcripts that must have been made of my bugged conversations. Where were they?

'I imagine,' said Mathur carelessly, as if it didn't really matter all that much, 'that they must have been put into a report.'

'And who got those reports?' I wanted to know.

'I imagine that the Home Secretary gets . . . got them.' He corrected himself quickly. But not quickly enough.

'GETS THEM?' I shrieked. 'You mean it's *still going on*?'

He tried to pacify me, but without success. 'No, Mantriji, not you, not now. *Now* he will be getting reports on current members of the Opposition.'

The mechanics were still unclear to me. 'Who gives these reports to the Home Secretary?' I demanded.

He shrugged. 'Intelligence Bureau, presumably.'

'You seem very calm about all this.'

He smiled. He was really getting right up my nose, the complacent . . . [*expletive deleted —Ed.*]

I certainly wasn't calm about it. I threw one of my real fits. I denounced the whole business. 'It is *horrifying*,' I insisted. 'An Indian citizen—in my case, a *distinguished* Indian citizen—one who has dedicated his life to the service of his fellow countrymen . . . and all the time those gloating, faceless bureaucrats are listening, undercover, to his every word. All his private calls.

101

His rows with his wife. His private arrangements with his accountant.' Perhaps I had gone too far—maybe the room was bugged! 'Not that I have anything I'd be ashamed to reveal, my life is an open book and all my accounts are perfectly clean.'

'Quite, quite,' agreed both Mathur and Kaul.

'But it's the principle of the thing!'

I stopped. I waited. The ball was in his court. Surely Mathur would have something to say. But no explanation or justification was forthcoming.

Mathur just sat there, head sympathetically inclined to one side, listening.

After he had said nothing for quite a long time, I realized that he *didn't* realize that the ball was in his court.

'Why?' I asked.

Mathur jumped, and focused his eyes in my direction. 'Why what?' he replied. 'Why surveillance, or why you?'

'Both.'

'In any case,' he smiled blandly, 'it's the same answer.'

My blood boiled. 'Then why,' I snapped, 'did you split it into two questions?'

There was no reply to that.

[*Shri Mathur could hardly explain to Suryaprakash Singh that he did not want to risk answering a question that Suryaprakash had not asked—Ed.*]

Then Mathur began his general explanation. 'I should have thought it was perfectly obvious. Before the election it was rumoured that you might be appointed Raksha Rajya Mantri [*Minister for Defence—Ed.*]. If the PM were to consider giving you Defence, you can surely see that it would be in the national interest for the Intelligence Bureau to satisfy itself that you were not a security risk?'

'But my privacy was invaded,' I pointed out.

He smiled his smuggest smile. 'Better than your country being invaded, Mantriji.'

I must say, I could see that point. There was a valid argument there.

But I was sure that Mathur had never experienced the feeling that I was feeling. And democracy is about the feelings and rights of the individual—that's what distinguishes a democracy from a dictatorship.

I said to him, 'Have *you* ever been under surveillance, Mathursaheb?'

He was astounded. 'Me?'

'You. You, Mathursaheb.'

He got on to his highest horse. 'I am a civil servant,' he said, as if that absolutely closed the discussion.

'And Secretaries are descended from Heaven,' I observed.

He was rattled, but he swiftly produced a counter-argument. 'One becomes a Secretary only after a lifetime of personal responsibility, reliability and integrity. The most rigorous selection procedures root out all but the most upright, honourable and discreet of public servants.'

I noted the emphasis on 'discreet'. The secrecy thing again, here openly acknowledged. I also noted that in giving this glowing description of Secretaries he thought that he was, in fact, describing himself. And I also noted that he had begged the question: even if Secretaries are never security risks, Mathur said that he had never been bugged. But he hasn't been a Secretary all his life, has he?

As Mathur had described the qualities of Secretaries in a way that argued that they need not be subject to surveillance, I inquired how he felt about ministers. It was as I expected.

'Ministers,' he said, 'have a whole range of dazzling qualities including . . . um . . . well, including an enviable intellectual suppleness and moral manoeuvrability.'

I invited him to explain himself.

'You can't trust ministers,' he said bluntly. I was appalled at his rudeness. 'I'm being quite candid now,' he added unnecessarily. Bloody insolent, I'd call it. 'I don't mean, by the way, that we can't trust *you*, Mantriji—of course we can. But in general terms ministers, unlike civil servants, are selected completely at random—by Prime Ministerial whim, in recognition of doubtful favours received, or to avoid appointing someone of real ability who might become a threat—not you, of course, Mantriji. You can certainly be trusted. You might almost be a civil servant yourself.'

[*Shri Mathur almost certainly meant this as a compliment. Indeed, the ultimate compliment. However, Suryaprakash should certainly have taken this as a hint that he might be house-trained. Regrettably, he allowed the flattery to get the better of him.—Ed.*]

I was mollified. I didn't think he was bullshitting.

I let him continue. 'Mantriji, would you trust every one of your Cabinet colleagues never to betray a confidence?'

I couldn't really give an answer to that, without appearing somewhat disloyal to my Cabinet colleagues.

'And what about all the Opposition front bench?' he asked. That was an easy one. 'You certainly can't trust that *jaahil* lot,' I exclaimed. [*Jaahil means uncivilized, therefore undependable, therefore untrustworthy—Ed.*]

'Quite so,' he said, checkmating me neatly, 'and you were on the Opposition front bench at the time.'

It has always been hard to win this kind of argument

with Mathur. But he's into winning arguments whereas I'm into getting things done!

So I cut the discussion short. I made my decision. Which was to stop all surveillance. It's a matter of principle.

He countered by informing me that this is a Home Ministry matter, and in many cases not within our purview.

This didn't bother me. I can certainly make it much more difficult in future. If I'm responsible for the apparatus, I intend to make myself responsible for some proper democratic safeguards for us all (before the apparatus can be used).

'Are you perhaps going to suggest, Mantriji,' he enquired sarcastically, 'that people will not be able to be put under secret surveillance until they've signed a form saying that they agree to it?'

I rose above it. 'No,' I said gently but firmly, 'I propose that we shall have a Select Committee of both Lok Sabha and Rajya Sabha to decide on every application. And no surveillance will be allowed to go on for more than two weeks without reapplying.'

Then I told him to set the wheels in motion.

He argued no further, but took his leave of me in a very frosty manner.

I was full of ideas today. After Mathur had stalked out I told Kaul to send a circular to each member of the Cabinet.

I also thought of planting a question from one of our MPs to the Home Minister. Something like: 'Will the Home Minister assure the Parliament that none of his Cabinet colleagues has ever been placed under government surveillance?' That will shake him. And it will bring the matter out into the open. We'll see if it's just a Home Ministry matter! I think not!

Finally, I asked Kaul to make an appointment for me to meet Shekhar Sengupta of the *Express* for a quick drink at the

India International Centre (IIC) one evening, later this week.

'What for?' Kaul wanted to know.

'First law of political indiscretion,' I replied. 'You always have a drink before you leak.'

[*Shekhar Sengupta was the Parliamentary Correspondent of the* Express. *This meant that he would probably have been their political editor or head of the paper's political staff. The Parliament Correspondent was a uniquely Indian system, the best way yet devised in any democracy for taming and muzzling the press.*

This is because it is hard to censor the press when it wants to be free, but easy if it gives up its freedom voluntarily.

There were in all 150 Parliamentary Correspondents, who had the special privilege of being able to mingle with MPs and Ministers in both Houses of Parliament. As journalists, however, they were—quite properly—not allowed to sit down on the benches. Neither were they allowed to report anything they saw— e.g. MPs hitting one another—nor anything they overheard.

One may ask: who stipulated what they were not allowed to do? Who made all these restrictions? Answer: The Parliamentary Correspondents themselves!

In return for the freedom of access to Ministers and MPs, they exercised the most surprising and elaborate self-censorship.

The correspondents received daily briefings from the Prime Minister's Press Secretary at the PMO, and weekly briefings from the Leader of the Lok Sabha and the Leader of the Opposition. All these briefings were unattributable.

The correspondents argued that, in return for their self-censorship, they would learn infinitely more about the government, its motives, and its plans. The politicians loved this system because they could leak any old rubbish, which the correspondents would generally swallow whole. As they had heard it in confidence, they believed it must be true.

The correspondent system was merely one example of the way in which the Indian political establishment dealt with potential danger or criticism—it would embrace the danger, and thus suffocate it.

The system certainly discouraged political journalists from going out and searching for a story, as they only had to sit in the Press Club (the bar exclusively reserved for the press, with the highest alcoholic consumption of any of the bars within the boundaries of Delhi—which was saying something!) and a 'leak' would come their way.

Finally, a word on leaks. Because there was no free access to information in Parliament, everybody leaked. Everybody knew there was no other way to make the wheels go round.

Equally, everybody pretended that leaking was underhand in some way. This is because discretion is the most highly valued talent in Parliament. Even above 'soundness'. Or perhaps discretion is the ultimate indication that you are 'sound'!

Whenever a 'leak' occurred there would be cries of moral indignation, and a leak enquiry would be set up by the Prime Minister. Such enquiries seldom reported at the end, for fear of the embarrassing result—most leaks came from the PMO (a euphemism), most budget leaks from South Block (another euphemism).—Ed.]

October 24th
I met Shekhar Sengupta in the IIC bar, as arranged, and leaked my plans for curtailing surveillance.

Sengupta seemed a little sceptical. He said it was a worthy cause but I'd never see it through. This made me all the more determined. I told him that I intended to see it through, and to tackle the Home Ministry on this matter in due course. I asked him if it would make a story—I knew it would, but journalists like to feel that their opinions are valuable.

Sengupta confirmed it would make a story: 'MINISTER FIGHTS FOR PHONE-TAP SAFEGUARDS—yes, there's something there.' He breathed deeply and drank two-thirds of a glass of beer.

I asked where they'd run it. He thought on page one, bottom lead at least. I was slightly disappointed.

'Not as main lead?'

'Well . . .' said Sengupta doubtfully. 'Can I attribute it? SURYAPRAKASH SINGH SPEAKS OUT!'

I squashed that at once.

'So where did I get the story?' asked Sengupta plaintively. 'I presume I can't say it was "officially announced" or a "government spokesman"?'

I told him he presumed right.

We silently pondered the other options.

'How about "sources close to the Minister"?' he asked after a minute or two.

'Hopeless,' I pointed out, 'I don't want *everybody* to know I told you. Isn't it possible for you to do a "speculation is growing in Parliamentary circles . . ."?'

Sengupta shook his head sadly. 'Bit weak,' he said.

'What about "unofficial spokesman"?' I suggested.

'That's really commonly used—anyway, it means neither the name nor the news is real,' replied Sengupta, smoking and contentedly adding to the pollution of the Delhi atmosphere. I choked quietly.

It was true. He had used it twice this week. I had noticed. 'Cabinet's leaking like a sieve, isn't it?'

He nodded. 'Yes—um . . . could we attribute it to a leading member of the sieve?' I looked at him. 'Er . . . Cabinet?' he corrected himself hastily.

I shook my head.

'How would you like to be an "informed source"?' he offered. That seemed a good idea. I hadn't been an informed source for some weeks.

'Okay,' I said. 'That's what I'll be.'

Sengupta chuckled. 'Quite a joke, isn't it?'

'What?' I asked blankly.

'Describing someone as "informed", when his Secretary is Mathursaheb.'

He bared his yellow teeth at me. I think it was a smile. I didn't smile back—I just bared my teeth at him.

October 25th

This evening I told Chandni about the surveillance we had been under. I thought she'd be as indignant as I was. But she didn't seem to care.

I tried to make her grasp the extent of the wrongdoing. 'Everything we said on the phone, everything we said to each other—all recorded. Transcribed. It's humiliating.'

'Yes, I see . . .' she said thoughtfully. 'It is a little humiliating that someone at Intelligence Bureau knows just how boring our life is.'

'What?'

'All will be revealed,' she said. 'Or has already been revealed. That what you talk about at home is what you talk about in public—the gross national product, the public sector borrowing requirement, the National Agenda . . .'

I explained that I didn't mean *that*. I meant that all our

private family talk had been overheard.

'Oh dear, yes,' said Chandni. 'I hadn't thought of that . . . "Where have you put my spectacles?" . . . "No, I thought you had them" . . . "No, I gave them to you" . . . My God, that could bring the government down!'

'Chandni,' I was cross. 'You're not taking this seriously.'

'Whatever gives you that idea?'

'You still haven't grasped how our privacy has been intruded upon. They might have heard what we say to each other . . . in bed.'

'Would it matter?' she asked, feigning surprise. 'Do you snore in code?'

I think she was trying to tell me something. Only last week she caused me great embarrassment when she was interviewed in some juvenile woman's magazine. They asked her if the earth moved when she went to bed with me. 'No,' she replied, 'not even the bed moves.'

Perhaps this was part of a campaign.

It was. She went on. 'Look, it's a long weekend this week. Let's go have a nice dinner, like we used to?'

My first thought was that I couldn't. Then I thought: why not? And I couldn't think of a reason. After all, even statesmen need to go out. I agreed.

'Let's go to Gaylords,' she said.

'Fine,' I said. 'But why Gaylords? It's not exactly a 5-star restaurant.'

She stared at me. 'It's only where you proposed to me.' Funny, I had forgotten the name of the place. I tried to remember what it looked like.

'It's where you first explained to me how a Bill becomes an Act in the Parliamentary legislative process.'

I remembered it well. 'Oh yes, I know the place then,' I said. Chandni turned towards her bedside lamp. 'Did you get that, boys?' she muttered into it.

[*A startling development took place on the following day. The Special Branch contacted Shri Mathur and Shri Kaul with the news that a terrorist hit list had been discovered, and Suryaprakash Singh's name appeared on it as a potential target. The list apparently was drawn up by a group calling itself the Youth for Direct Action Group. —Ed.*]

Kaul Saheb recalls:
We could not imagine who on earth could possibly want to assassinate Suryaprakash Singh. He was so harmless.

Nevertheless, Mathursaheb and I were fully agreed that it was not possible to take risks with the Mantriji's life, and so the whole paraphernalia of security would have to be brought out to protect him.

[*Suryaprakash's diary continues —Ed.*]

October 27th
Kaul greeted me like a mother hen this morning. He asked after my health with an earnest and solicitous attitude.

I thought perhaps it was because I was a little late at the office. I hadn't slept too well—'I feel like death,' I remarked.

Kaul whispered to Mathur, 'Perhaps that's just as well,' a comment which I did not understand at the time but which I now regard as having been in the poorest of taste.

I was actually rather cheerful. My leak had worked. A story had appeared in the *Express*: SINGH MOVES TO CURB PHONE TAPS.

111

now regard as having been in the poorest of taste.

I was actually rather cheerful. My leak had worked. A story had appeared in the *Express*: SINGH MOVES TO CURB PHONE TAPS. I was described as an informed source, as agreed, and Sengupta had not taken a by-line—the story was 'From Our Political Staff'.

Mathur wondered audibly where they had got the information, and stared at me. Naturally I admitted nothing.

[*It has been said that the ship of state is the only type of ship that leaks from the top —Ed.*]

'Anyway,' I added, 'this leak only confirms my determination to act on this matter.'

Mathur asked me if I had considered all the implications. This is generally the Administrative Service way of asking me if I realized that I was talking rubbish. In this case, as it was to turn out, I had not quite considered all the implications.

So I replied that free citizens have a right to privacy. An absolute right.

How could I have said such a thing?

But I didn't know then what I knew just five minutes later. Those fellows hadn't told me.

'Suppose . . .' suggested Mathur smoothly, 'suppose Intelligence Bureau had reason to suspect that these "free citizens" were, shall we say to take a purely hypothetical example, planning to assassinate a Minister of the Cabinet?'

I made a little speech. I spoke of the freedom of the Indian people, and how this is more important than the lives of a few Mantris. I said that freedom is indispensable, whereas ministers are expendable. 'Men in public life must expect to be the targets of cranks and fanatics. A Mantri has the duty to set his own life at naught, to stand up and say, "Here I am, do your worst!" and not cower in terror behind electronic equipment and secret

microphones and all the hideous apparatus of the police state.'
Me and my big mouth.

Mathur and Kaul looked at each other. The former tried to speak but I made it clear that I would brook no arguments.

'No Mathursaheb, I don't want to hear any more about it. You deal in evasions and secrets. But politicians in a free country must be seen to be the champions of freedom and truth.'

Mathur succeeded in interrupting.

'Mantriji,' he insisted, 'you *must* allow me to say one more thing on this matter.'

I told him that he might say one sentence, but he should keep it brief.

'The Special Branch has found your name on a hit list,' he said.

I thought I must have misheard. 'What?' I said.

'The Special Branch has found your name on a hit list,' he repeated.

This made no sense. A hit list? Why me?

'A hit list?' I asked. 'What do you mean, a hit list?'

'An assassination list,' he said.

He really is a fool. 'I know what you mean by a hit list,' I said, 'but . . . what do you mean?'

Mathur was now as baffled as I.

'I don't know how I can express it more clearly, Mantriji,' he said plaintively.

Obviously, I wanted him to explain things like what the list was, where it came from, why I was on it—my mind was racing with dozens of unanswered questions, that's why I was so inarticulate.

Mathur tried to answer what he thought I was asking him.

'To put it absolutely bluntly, Mantriji, confidential

investigations have revealed the existence of certain documents whose provenance is currently unestablished, but whose effect if realized would be to create a Cabinet vacancy and precipitate a by-election.'

I didn't know what he meant. I asked him.

'You are on a hit list, Mantriji.'

We were going round in circles. 'Who . . .?' I spluttered. 'What . . .?'

'Ah,' he said. 'I see. It is the Youth for Direct Action. A new urban terrorist group, apparently.'

My bowels were turning to water. 'But what have they got against me?' I whispered.

Kaul reminded me of the vague rumours recently of a Cabinet reshuffle, and that my name had been mentioned in one or two of the papers in connection with the Ministry of Defence.

I asked who they could be, these urban terrorists. Kaul and Mathur just shrugged.

'Hard to say, Mantriji. It could Osama bin Laden, Harkat-ul-Ansar, Dawood Ibrahim. It could be homegrown loonies—Marx-vaadi, Lenin-vaadi, or Naxal-vaadi. Or it might be the LTTE, North-East rebels or freelance terrorists for all we know.'

'In any case,' added Kaul, 'they're all interconnected really. This could simply be a new group of freelance killers. The Special Branch doesn't know where to start.'

That was *very* encouraging, I must say! I couldn't get over the cool, callous, unemotional way in which they were discussing some maniacs who were trying to kill me. I tried to grasp at straws.

'There's a list of names, is there? You said a list? Not just me?'

'Not just you, Mantriji,' Mathur confirmed.

I said that I supposed that there were hundreds of names on it. 'Just three,' said Mathur.

'Three?'

I was in a state of shock, I think. Or panic. One of those. I just sat there unable to think or speak. My mouth had completely dried up.

As I tried to say something, anything, the phone rang. Kaul answered it. Apparently somebody called Joint Director Vinay Kumar from Special Branch, Intelligence Bureau had come to brief me.

Kaul went to get him. As he left he turned to me and said in a kindly fashion, 'Try looking at it this way, Mantriji—it's always nice to be on a shortlist. At least they know who you are.'

I gave him a withering look, and he hurried out.

Mathur filled in the background. The Special Branch had apparently informed the Home Secretary (the usual procedure) who had recommended detectives to protect me.

I didn't see how they could protect me. How could detectives protect me from an assassin's bullet? Nobody can. Everybody knows that.

I said this to Mathur. I suppose I hoped he'd disagree—but he didn't. 'Look at it this way,' he responded. 'Even if detectives cannot protect anyone, they do ensure that the assassin is brought to justice. After the victim has been gunned down.'

Thanks a lot!

Kaul brought in Vinay Kumar. He was a tall thin cadaverous-looking individual, with a slightly nervous flinching manner. He didn't really inspire confidence.

I decided that I had to put on a brave show. Chin up, stiff upper lip, pull myself together, that sort of thing. I had been

talking a lot about leadership. Now I had to prove to them—
and myself—that I was bravery material.

I smiled reassuringly at the Joint Director, as he
offered to brief me on the standard hazards and routine
precautions. 'I don't really have to take these things too
seriously, do I?' I asked in a cavalier manner.

'Well, sir, in a sense, it's up to you, but we do advise . . .'

I interrupted. 'Look, I can see that some people might get
into a frightful state about this but, well, it's the job, isn't it? All
in a day's work.'

Joint Director Vinay Kumar gazed at me strangely. 'I admire
your courage, sir,' he said as if he really thought I were a *pukka*
[*thoroughbred —Ed.*] idiot.

I decided I had done enough of the stiff upper lip. I let him
speak. 'Okay, shoot,' I said. It was an unfortunate turn of phrase.

'Read this,' he said, and thrust a xeroxed typescript into
my hand. 'This will tell you all you need to know. Study it,
memorize it, and keep it to yourself.'

[*A copy of the document handed to Suryaprakash follows. It is
self-explanatory —Ed.*]

SECURITY PRECAUTIONS

Assassination hazards fall broadly into four categories:
i.   BULLETS
ii. BOMBS
iii. POISONS
iv. ACCIDENTS (so-called)

There is also the possibility of gassing, throttling, stabbing, drowning, garroting and ritual disembowelling, but most of these are comparatively infrequent in India.

i.   BULLETS

Snipers can be found in various locations:
a.   A high building
b.   A car travelling beside your car
c.   Stealing up close to you in a crowd
d.   At your front door as an unexpected caller
e.   In a parked van concealing a marksman
f.   Thrusting a revolver through your car window etc.

Precautions

a.   Avoid crowds
b.   Keep away from windows (Bullet-proof net curtains will be provided at your home and your office)
c.   Never answer your own front door
d.   Keep your car window up, windows and doors locked while you are driving
e.   Never draw up at traffic lights on the pavement side
f.   If a car pulls across in front of you, do not ram it in the

middle. Aim for one of the axles and sweep it aside.

N.B. Intially, Special Branch Police Officers will not only answer your front door for you, but will give all available protection and cover alarms, twenty-four-hour patrols by six or seven Black Cat Commandos, special locks, phone taps etc.

ii. BOMBS
a. Car-bombs—use regulation issue mirror at the end of a long pole, in order to check thoroughly the underside of your chassis each morning, and on any occasion on which the car has been left unattended.
b. Letter/parcel bombs—never open any yourself.

N.B. For the time being all your mail will be redirected.

iii. POISONS
a. Gifts of food and drink, chocolates, mithai etc.—treat with suspicion
b. Check soft drink bottle tops for hypodermic holes
c. Avoid strangers approaching you with umbrellas—(the ferrule jabbed in the calf/thigh method).

iv. ACCIDENTS
a. Falling:
1. Pavements
2. Rivers
3. Sea-fronts
4. Railway platforms

118

Avoid trains: large crowds make it too easy.

b. Electrocution:
View with suspicion:
  1. The television set
  2. The fan, cooler
  3. The toaster
  4. The hi-fi
  5. The air-conditioner (these can also be used as denotation devices for booby-trap bombs).

c. Windows:
If pushed from a high window with iron railings below, try and fall on your head. It's quicker.

I read the document through. It seemed to me as though I had little chance of survival. But I must continue to have courage.

After Joint Director Vinay Kumar had left, I asked Mathur how the police would find these terrorists before they found me. That seems to be my only hope.

Mathur remarked that telephone tapping and electronic surveillance of all possible suspects is the best way of picking these fellows up.

'But,' he added cautiously, 'that does incur intolerable intrusion upon individual privacy.'

I carefully considered the implications of this comment. And then I came to the conclusion. A slightly different conclusion, although I think that perhaps he had misunderstood what I had been saying earlier.

I carefully considered the implications of this comment. And then I came to the conclusion. A slightly different conclusion, although I think that perhaps he had misunderstood what I had been saying earlier.

I explained that, on the other hand, if the people's elected representatives are to represent the people, it follows that any attack on these elected representatives is, *in itself*, an attack on freedom and democracy. The reason is clear. Such threats strike at the very heart of the people's inalienable democratic right to be governed by the leaders of their choice. Therefore, the safety of these leaders must be protected by every possible means—however much we might regret the necessity for doing so or the measures that we may be forced to take.

I explained all this to Mathur. He was in complete agreement—although I didn't care for his choice of words. 'Beautifully argued, Mantriji,' he replied. 'My view exactly—or else *Ram naam satya hai*.' [*Colloquial Hindi phrase meaning you are a dead duck —Ed.*]

Later today there was a slight embarrassment.

My petition arrived.

The petition against phone tapping and electronic surveillance, the one that I started a year and a half ago when I was in the Opposition and editor of *Manav Adhikar*. Kaul wheeled into my room a huge office trolley loaded with piles of exercise books and reams of paper. It now has ten lakh signatures. A triumph of organization and commitment, and what the hell do I do with it?

It is now clear to me—now that I have the *full* facts which you cannot get when in Opposition, of course—that surveillance is an indispensable weapon in the fight against organized terror and crime.

Kaul understood. He offered to file the petition.

I wasn't sure that filing it was the answer. We had acknowledged receipt from the deputation—they would never ask to see it again. And they would imagine that it was in safe hands since I'm the one who began it all.

I told him to shred it. 'Kaul,' I said, 'we must make certain that no one ever finds it again.'

'In that case,' replied Kaul, 'I'm sure it would be best to file it.'

October 30th

I've just had the most awful long weekend of my life.

Chandni and I went Gaylords for dinner. It seemed as though the whole of the Intelligence Bureau came too.

'How many for dinner?' asked the waiter as we came in. 'Seven,' said Chandni acidly. The weekend was not working out as she had expected.

The waiter offered us a nice table for two by the window, but it was vetoed by a Black Cat commando. 'No, that's not safe,' he muttered to me, and turned to a colleague. 'We've chosen that table over there for the target.'

Target! So Chandni and I were escorted to a cramped little table in a poky little corner next to the kitchen doors. They banged open and shut right beside us, throughout our meal.

As we sat down I was briefed by one of the detectives. 'You sit here. Constable Ghatge will sit over there, watching the kitchen door—that's your escape route. We don't expect any assassins to be among the kitchen staff as we only booked in here late afternoon. I'll sit by the window. And if you do hear any gunshots, just dive under the table and I'll take care of it.'

I'm sure he meant to be reassuring. I informed him that I wasn't a bit worried. Then I heard a loud report close to my head, and I crashed under the table.

An utterly humiliating experience—some seconds later I stuck my head out and realized that a champagne bottle had just been opened for the next table. I had to pretend that I had just been practising.

By this time, with all this talk of escape routes, assassins in the kitchen and so forth, I had gone right off my food. So had Chandni.

When we went for a quiet afternoon stroll through the park the next day, the whole place was swarming with Black Cats.

They kept nice and close to us—very protective, but impossible for Chandni and me to discuss anything but the weather. They all look the other way—not, I hasten to add, out of courtesy or respect for our privacy, but to see if they could spot any potential attacker leaping towards me over the roses.

We stuck it out for nearly two days. We went to the cinema on Saturday evening, but that made Chandni even more furious. She had wanted to see *Four Weddings and a Funeral* but in the end we went to a Hindi film—I knew that none of the detectives liked English films, and it didn't seem fair to drag them along to one.

Chandni was black with rage because I had put their choice first. When she put it like that, I saw what she meant. The detectives were very fed up with us when we walked out halfway through the film.

Finally, back in our home, we lay in our own beds, still rigid with tension, still unable to go to the toilet without some constable examining it first, still with detectives knocking on the bedroom door and barging straight in while saying, 'May I just check your windows, sir,' but with the additional pleasures of dogs barking and searchlights lighting up the whole room at intervals of twenty-nine seconds.

I told Chandni, pathetically trying to make the best of it all, that she'd soon get used to being a famous man's wife. She said she would sooner get used to it than become a famous man's widow.

October 31st

Today I was back in the office and trying to handle a difficult interview with Shekhar Sengupta, who had somehow got wind of the petition. He seemed to find it extraordinary that I had now suppressed the petition that I started the year before last. Of course, he didn't know that my changed circumstances had made me see the whole matter of surveillance in a fresher and clearer way.

'I don't follow,' he complained. 'You say you're out to stop bugging and phone tapping. And now you get this petition. Ten lakh signatures. A terrific boost to your case. And you won't even give me a quote saying you welcome it?'

I made an unshakable resolve to stay silent. Anything I said was liable to be quoted. You can't ever trust the press.

'What about making a promise to implement its main recommendations?'

I realized that I had to break my unshakable resolve. 'Well you see, Sengupta,' I began in my most condescending manner, 'things aren't that simple.'

'Why not?' he asked.

'Security considerations,' I said.

'There always were,' he said. 'But you said yourself that "security" is the last excuse of a desperate bureaucrat.'

Irritating fellow. I resolved to stay silent again.

Then Sengupta said, 'Okay. I think I'll make it an even bigger story. MANTRI REJECTS HIS OWN PETITION.'

My resolve shook again. '*Arre bhai* Sengupta,' I blurted out, 'don't be silly.'

'Are you accepting the petition or rejecting it?' he asked, giving me a simple choice.

'No,' I replied carefully.

Then it transpired that he did know all my circumstances. 'My editor wants me to ask if being on the Youth for Direct Action hit list has altered your views in any way.'

Of course it has! Obviously! I'd be a complete fool if it hadn't. 'Certainly not,' I said. 'What an absurd idea! Never had occurred to me till you mentioned it just now.'

He didn't believe me but he couldn't prove anything. 'But how else am I to explain this sudden change of tune?'

I was getting a bit desperate by then, but thank God Kaul knocked on the door and appeared. Saved by the bell. He told me Mathur wanted a word with me.

Mathur came in. Sengupta didn't leave till I asked him if he minded. And he didn't leave the building—he just said he'd wait outside till we had finished.

Mathur asked me if I had had a good weekend. Sadistic fellow. He must have known what my weekend would be like, with half the Special Branch present—all those romantic commandos with guns under their armpits. I told him so.

He nodded sympathetically. 'The burdens of office,' he said.

'This can't go on!' I said. Why can't I keep my big mouth shut?

'I'm glad you said that,' he replied smoothly, 'because it isn't going to.' My jaw dropped open. 'We've just heard from the Special Branch that your protection is being withdrawn.'

Withdrawn? I was appalled. I thought he had misunderstood

me. I asked why?

'The police have suffered an acute personnel establishment shortfall.'

I was about to ask if anybody was hurt, when I realized what he meant. Short-staffed. He meant short-staffed! And because the police were short-staffed they were going to allow me to be killed? I was horrified.

'There is a much more real and dangerous threat to the Sri Lankan Foreign Minister who is expected here tomorrow,' he continued.

Much more real and dangerous? More real and dangerous to *him*, maybe. I searched desperately for an argument for them to protect me rather than him. 'He's Sri Lanka's Minister,' I said. 'I'm Indian!'

Then Mathur revealed further reasons why my protection was to be withdrawn.

'In fact, Mantriji, the Special Branch is confident that the threat to your life has diminished.'

Naturally I was anxious to know how they could be so bloody confident.

'Surveillance, Mantriji. They overheard a conversation.' Mathur seemed reluctant to tell me. I told him to spit it out. I had a right to know, and I wanted a straight answer!

He nodded, and then went into his normal mumbo-jumbo. God knows what he said. I couldn't unravel it.

Kaul Saheb recalls:

I remember what Mathursaheb said because I minuted it at the time. He explained that in view of the somewhat nebulous and inexplicit nature of Suryaprakash's remit and the arguably marginal and peripheral nature of Suryaprakash's influence on the central deliberations and decisions within the political process, there would be a case for restructuring their action priorities in such a way as to eliminate Suryaprakash's liquidation from their immediate agenda.

[*Suryaprakash's diary continues —Ed.*]

So I asked him to put it into English. He then said that the Youth for Direct Action had apparently decided that I wasn't really important enough for it to be worth assassinating me.

He put it as gently as he could, I could see that. Even so, it was a bit of a blow. Not that they had decided not to assassinate me, of course, but a bit of a blow to my pride nonetheless.

I asked Mathur what he thought of this new situation. 'I don't agree with them, of course,' he said.

'You mean,' I asked, 'you think I *should* be assassinated?'

'No, no.'

'You mean, I'm not important enough?'

'Yes. *No*! I mean you *are* important enough but they shouldn't assassinate you anyway.' He breathed a sigh of relief.

Anyway, it seemed I was off the hook, and perhaps that's all to the good. I mean, there's no point in being important but dead, is there? But, if even terrorist loonies doubt my value to the government, there's clearly some image-building to be done right away.

Kaul then asked me if I would finish my interview with Sengupta. Of course, I was delighted to.

He was ushered in, and I opened up right away. I told Kaul to bring the petition along on the trolley, so that Sengupta could see how big it was.

Kaul said, 'The petition? But I thought you said . . .'

'Yes I did,' I interrupted hastily. 'Could you get it, Kaul?'
He still looked blank. 'Antennae, Kaul,' I explained.

Light dawned. 'Ah. Yes. Indeed, Mantriji,' he said quickly.
'You mean, I'm to get the petition that you said you were so
pleased with?'

The boy's learning.

Sengupta demanded an answer to his various questions. I
told him to sit down. Then I told him that I welcomed the
petition, warmly. That it is not just something you sweep under
the carpet.

'And as for hit lists,' I concluded. 'Well—Mantris are
expendable, but freedom is indispensable. Isn't that so,
Mathursaheb?'

'Ji Mantriji,' replied my smiling Secretary, right on cue.

5

The Foreign Visit

November 6th

I am finding that it is impossible to get through all the work. The diary is always full, speeches constantly have to be written and delivered, and files full of papers, documents, memos, minutes, submissions and letters have to be read carefully every night. And this is only *part* of my work.

Here I am, attempting to function as a sort of managing director of a very large and important business and I have no previous experience either of the Department's work or, in fact, of management of any kind. A career in politics is no preparation for government.

And, as if becoming managing director of a huge corporation were not enough, I am also attempting to do it part-time. I constantly have to leave the MAA to attend debates in Parliament, to vote, to go to Cabinet and Cabinet committees and party executive meetings, and I now see that it is not possible to do this job properly or even adequately. I am rather depressed.

Can anyone seriously imagine the chairman of a company leaping like a madman out of a meeting in his office every time a bell rings, no matter when, at any time of the afternoon or evening, racing like P.T. Usha to another building, rushing through a lobby, and running back to his office to continue the meeting? This is what I have to do every time the voting bell rings. Sometimes six or seven times in one day. And do I have any idea at all what I'm voting for? Of course I don't. How could I?

Today I arrived in the office and was immediately cast down by the sight of my in-tray. Full to overflowing. The out-tray was completely empty.

Kaul was patiently waiting for me to read some piece of impenetrable prose that he had dug up, in answer to the question I had asked him yesterday: what are my actual powers in various far-flung parts of India, such as Nagaland and Lakshwadeep?

He proudly offered me a document. It said: 'Notwithstanding the provisions of subsection 3 of Section A of Article 16 of the Administrative Procedures (Nagaland) Act 1978, it has been agreed that, insofar as the implementation of the statutory provisions is concerned, the resolution of anomalies and uncertainties between responsible departments shall fall within the purview of the Minister for Administrative Affairs.'

I gazed blankly at it for what seemed an eternity. My mind just seemed to cloud over, as it used to at school when faced with geometric theorems or physics. I longed to sleep. And it was only 9.15 a.m. I asked Kaul what it meant. He seemed puzzled by the question. He glanced at his own copy of the document.

'Well, Mantriji,' he began, 'it means that notwithstanding the provisions of subsection 3 of Section A of Article 16 of . . .'

I interrupted him. 'Don't read it to me,' I said. 'I've just read it. What does it *mean*?'

Kaul gazed blankly at me. 'What it says, Mantriji.' He wasn't trying to be unhelpful. I realized that Parliament papers, though totally incomprehensible to normal people, are written in the everyday language of the Parliament Man.

INTERDEPARTMENTAL COMMITTEE ON
ADMINISTRATIVE PROCEDURES

Chairman   Shri Rajnath Mathur

Present   Shri Jagat Narain Mittal
                Shri Behram Rastogi
                Smt Ramgopal Goenka
                Shri Akash Dalmia
                Shri Tapas Mukherji

Secretary   Ms Nagpal

1. The Minutes of the previous
meeting were read and agreed.
2. Matters arising:
(i) Notwithstanding the provisions of
subsection 3 of Section A of Article 16 of
the Administrative Procedures (Nagaland)
Act 1978, it has been agreed that, insofar
as the implementation of the statutory
provisions is concerned, the resolution of
anomalies and uncertainties between
responsible departments shall fall within
the purview of the Minister for
Administrative Affairs.

/over

Minutes of a Meeting held at the Department of
  Administrative Affairs on October 31st

133

Kaul hurried out into the Private Office and brought me the diary.

[The Private Office is the office immediately adjoining the Minister's office. In it are the desks of the Private Secretary and the three or four Assistant Private Secretaries, including the Diary Secretary—a full-time job. Adjoining the inner Private Office is the outer Private Office, containing about twelve people, all secretarial and clerical staff, processing replies to parliamentary questions, letters, etc. Access to the Minister's office is through the Private Office. Throughout the day everyone, whether outsiders or members of the Department, continually come and go through the Private Office. The Private Office is, therefore, somewhat public.—Ed.]

'May I remind you, Mantriji, that you are seeing a deputation from the AITUC in fifteen minutes, and from the INTUC half an hour after that, and the SITU-walas at twelve noon,' Kaul said.

My feeling of despair increased. 'What do they all want—roughly?' I asked.

'They are all worried about the machinery for inflation, deflation and reflation,' Kaul informed me. What do they think I am? A Minister of the Indian Government or a bicycle pump?

I indicated the in-tray. 'When am I going to get through all this correspondence?' I asked Kaul wearily.

Kaul said, 'You *do* realize, Mantriji, that you don't actually *have* to?'

I had realized no such thing. This sounded good.

Kaul continued, 'If you want, we can simply draft an official *jawab* to any letter.'

'What's an official reply?' I wanted to know.

'It just says,' Kaul explained, '"the Minister has asked me to thank you for your letter". Then *we* reply. Something like: "The

134

matter is under consideration." Or even, if we feel so inclined, "under active consideration"!'

'What's the difference between "under consideration" and "under active consideration"?' I asked.

'"Under consideration" means we've lost the file. "Under active consideration" means we're trying to find it!'

I think this might have been one of Kaul's little jokes. But I'm not absolutely certain.

Kaul was eager to tell me what I had to do in order to lighten the load of my correspondence. 'You just transfer every letter from your in-tray to your out-tray. You put a brief note in the margin if you want to see the reply. If you don't, you need never see or hear of it again.'

I was stunned. My secretary was sitting there, seriously telling me that if I move a pile of unanswered letters from one side of my desk to the other, that is all I have to do?

So I asked Kaul, 'Then what is a Mantri for?'

'To make policy decisions,' he replied fluently. 'When you have decided the policy, we can carry it out.'

It seems to me that if I do not read the letters I will be somewhat ill-informed, and that therefore the number of so-called policy decisions will be reduced to a minimum.

Worse: I would not *know* which were the decisions that I needed to take. I would be dependent on my officials to tell me. I suspect that there would not be very many decisions left.

So I asked Kaul, 'How often are policy decisions needed?'

Kaul hesitated. 'Well . . . from time to time, Mantriji,' he replied in a kindly way.

I decided that enough was enough. 'Kaul,' I said firmly, '*this* government governs. It does not just preside like our predecessors did. When a nation's been going downhill you need someone to get into the driving seat, and put his foot on the accelerator.'

'I think perhaps you mean the brake, Mantriji,' said Kaul.

I simply do not know whether this earnest young man is being helpful, or is putting me down.

November 7th
There was a meeting this morning in my office about the official visit to India of the President of the Republic of Chagos. I had never even heard of Chagos.

Kaul gave me the brief last night. I found it in the third file. But I had very little time to study it. I asked Mathur to tell me about Chagos—like, where is it?

'It's right underneath India on the map, Mantriji. It's the pink drop three inches below India . . . that one,' he said, pointing to the map. 'Population one lakh.'

I can't see what Chagos has got to do with us. With a population of just one lakh, it is smaller than Chandni Chowk in Delhi. Surely this is a Foreign and External Affairs job. But it was explained to me that there was an administrative problem because the President is overseas for a health check-up. At the same time, the PM will be in the North-East.

'Its a protocol call, Mantriji,' said Mathur. Kaul started. Any reference to calls always startles Kaul, but Mathur never seems to notice.

Anyway, this surprised me. I had always thought that State Visits were arranged years in advance. I said so.

'This is not a State Visit,' said Mathur. 'It is a Head of Government visit.'

I asked if the President of Chagos wasn't the Head of State? Mathur said that indeed he was, but also the Head of Government.

I said that, if he's merely coming as Head of State, I didn't see why the PM had to greet him. Mathur said that it was because *he* is the Head of Government. I couldn't see the logic. Mathur says that the Head of Government must greet a Head of Government, even if the visiting Head of Government is not *here* as a Head of Government but only as a Head of State.

Then Kaul decided to explain. 'It's all a matter of *Heads*, Mantriji,' he said.

'Heads?' I was becoming even more confused.

'Yes,' said Kaul, 'he's coming here as the Head of Government. He is the Head of State, too, but it's not a State Visit because he's not coming as the Head of State, but protocol demands that even though he is coming as the Head of Government, he must still be met by . . .' I could see his desperate attempt to avoid either mixing metaphors or abandoning his elaborately constructed speech, '. . . the Head,' he finished in triumph.

I said that I had never heard of Chagos anyway, and I didn't know why we were bothering with an official visit from this *boond-barabar desh* ['*boond-barabar desh*'—*country the size of a tear-drop, obviously used pejoratively in Hindi —Ed.*].

Mathur and Kaul went visibly pale. I looked at their faces, frozen in horror.

'Mantriji,' said Mathur, 'I beg you not to refer to it as a *boond-barabar desh*. It is an LDC.'

LDC is a new one for me. It seems that Chagos is what used to be called an Underdeveloped Country. However, this term has apparently become offensive, so then it was called a Developing Country. This term apparently was patronizing. So it became a Less Developed Country—or LDC, for short.

Mathur tells me that I *must* be clear on my international terminology, or else I could do irreparable damage.

137

It seems, in a nutshell, that the term Less Developed Countries is not yet causing offence to anyone. When it does, we are immediately ready to replace the term LDC with HRRC. This is short for Human Resource-Rich Countries, like India. In other words, these are places that are grossly overpopulated, where money is in short supply and who are looking for international aid. However, Chagos is *not* an HRRC. Nor is it one of the 'Haves' or 'Have-not' nations—apparently we no longer use those terms either, we talk about the North–South dialogue instead. In fact it seems that Chagos is a 'Will Have' nation, if there were such a term, and if it were not to cause offence to our Afro-Asian, or Third-World, or Non-Aligned-Nation brothers.

'Chagos will have a huge amount of oil in a couple of years from now,' confided Mathur.

'Oh I see,' I said. 'So it's not a BBD at all.'

Mathur was baffled. It gave me pleasure to baffle him for once. 'BBD?' he enquired carefully.

'*Boond-barabar desh*,' I explained. Mathur and Kaul jumped. They looked profoundly shocked. They glanced nervously around to check that I had not been overheard. They were certainly not amused. How silly—anyone would think my office was bugged! [*Perhaps it was —Ed.*]

November 8th
On my way to work this morning I had an inspiration.

At my meeting with Mathur yesterday it had been left for him to make arrangements to get the PM down from the North-East to meet the Chagos President. But this morning I remembered that we have three by-elections pending in three North-East constituencies, as a result of the death of one member who was so surprised that his constituents re-elected him in spite of his corruption and dishonesty that he had a heart attack and died, and as a result of the elevation of two other members to the Rajya Sabha on the formation of the new government. [*The Rajya Sabha and/or the heart attack are, of course, the two most usual rewards for a career of corruption and dishonesty —Ed.*]

I called Mathur to my office. 'The PM,' I announced, 'does not have to come down from the North-East at all.'

There was a slight pause.

'Are you proposing, Mantriji,' said Mathur in a pained manner, 'that the PM and the President should exchange official greetings by telephone?'

'No.'

'Then,' said Mathur, even more pained, 'perhaps you just want them to shout very loudly.'

'Not that either,' I said cheerfully. 'We will hold the official visit in the North-East. Guwahati.'

Mathur replied instantly.

'Out of the question,' he said.

'Mathursaheb,' I said, 'are you sure you've given this idea due consideration?'

'It's not our decision,' he replied. 'It's an External Affairs matter.'

I was ready for this. I spent last night studying that wretched document which had caused me so much trouble day before yesterday. 'I don't think so,' I said, and produced the file with a fine flourish. 'Notwithstanding the provisions of subsection 3 blah blah blah . . . administrative procedures blah blah blah . . . shall fall within the purview of the Minister for Administrative Affairs.' I sat back and watched.

Mathur was stumped. 'Yes, but . . . why do you want to do this?' he asked.

'It saves the PM a pointless journey. And there are three North-East by-elections coming up. We'll hold them as soon as the visit is over.'

He suddenly went rather cool. 'Mantriji, we do not hold Head of Government visits for party political reasons, but for reasons of State and Government.'

He had a point there. I had slipped up a bit, but I managed to justify it. 'But my plan will really work for the whole country. The North-East has felt that since 1947, they have been neglected compared to the other regions. We will show them that they are an equal part of the country. He *is* PM of the North-East too. And the North-East is full of marginal constit . . .' I stopped myself just in time, I think, '. . . backward areas.'

But Mathur was clearly hostile to the whole brilliant notion. 'I hardly think, Mantriji,' he sneered, clambering onto his highest horse and looking down his nose at me, 'I hardly think we can exploit our PM by involving him in, if you will forgive the phrase, squalid vote-grabbing petty politics.'

I don't think there's anything squalid about vote-grabbing. I'm democratic and proud of it and that's what democracy is all about! But I could see that I had to think up a better reason (for Administrative Service consumption, at least) or else this excellent plan would be blocked somehow. So I asked Mathur why the President of Chagos was coming to India.

'For an exchange of views on matters of mutual interest,' was the reply. Why does this man insist on speaking in the language of official circulars? Or can't he help it?

'*Achcha*, now tell me why he's coming,' I asked with exaggerated patience. I was prepared to keep asking until I got the real answer.

'He's here to place a huge order with the Indian government

140

for offshore oil and gas drilling equipment.'

Perfect! I went in for the kill. 'And where can he see all our offshore equipment? Not in Connaught Place in Delhi but, in fact, in the North-East.'

Mathur tried to argue. 'Yes, but . . . the administrative problems . . .' he began. I interrupted grandly, 'Administrative problems are what this whole Department was created to solve. I'm sure you can do it, Mathursaheb.'

'But Guwahati's so remote.' He was whining and complaining now. I knew I had got him on the run. 'Not all that remote,' I said, and pointed to the map hanging on the wall. 'It's that pink bit, about a foot away from here.'

Mathur was not amused. 'Very charming, Mantriji,' he said. But even that did not crush me.

'It is going to be Guwahati,' I said with finality. 'That is my policy decision. That's what I'm here for, right Kaul?'

Kaul didn't want to take sides against Mathur, or against me. He was stuck. 'Um . . .' he said.

I dismissed Mathur, and told him to get on with making the arrangements. He stalked out of my office. Kaul's eyes remained glued to the floor.

Kaul is *my* Private Secretary and, as such, is apparently supposed to be on my side. On the other hand, his future lies with the Department, which means that he has to be on Mathur's side. I don't see how he can possibly be on both sides. Yet, apparently, only if he succeeds in this task that is, by definition, impossible, will he continue his rapid rise to the top. It's all very puzzling. I must try and find out if I can trust him.

November 9th
Had a little chat with Kaul today on our way to address a

conference of Municipal Treasurers.

Kaul warned me that Mathur's next move, over this North-East business, would be to set up an interdepartmental committee to investigate and report.

I regard the interdepartmental committee as the last refuge of a desperate bureaucrat. When you can't find any argument against something you don't want, you set up an interdepartmental committee to strangle it. Slowly. I said so to Kaul. He agreed.

'It's for the same reason that politicians set up Justice Committees,' said Kaul. I began to see why he's a high-flyer.

I decided to ask Kaul what Mathur *really* has against the idea.

Kaul explained. Apparently the problem is that Mathur likes to go to the embassies, all dressed up in his suits and *bandh-galas* [*Indian formal dress, with Nehru-collars —Ed.*] and medals. But in the North-East there will be no scope for all that—not so many colourful evenings with continental food and drinks. Not so many for Mathur, anyway, only for the Co-ordinating Officers for the North-Eastern States. Mathur might not probably even go to Guwahati.

I had never given the ceremonial aspect of all this any thought at all. But according to Kaul all the glitter is frightfully important to Secretaries. I asked Kaul if Mathur had lots of medals to wear.

'Quite a few,' Kaul told me. 'Of course he got his Indo-German friendship award, World Citizen Charter Award and India-Nepal Co-operation awards a long time ago. But there are rumours that he might get his Padma Shree in the next few months.'

'How did you hear that?' I asked. I thought these awards were top secret.

'I heard it on the grapevine,' said Kaul. I suppose, if Mathur doesn't get his Padma Shree, we'll hear about it on the sour-grapevine.

[Shortly after this conversation a note was sent by Shri Mathur to Kaul. As usual Shri Mathur wrote in the margin.—Ed.]

Kaul

Have spoken to the Sec. at the MEA about official visit to Guwahati.

Unfortunately, our Minister had already spoken to the External Affairs Minister. I gather they are chums.

It appears that the Cabinet is utterly united on this matter. They have blatantly issued writs for three by-elections on the day of the visit.

It seems that the Chagos Republic High Commission is rather small and cramped. V. little space at the dinner, and I shall not be going. Rather relieved, really.

However, Sec. at MEA hinted that there are rumblings in the interior. Our men in Lakshwadeep are expecting trouble in Chagos. Possibly a coup d'état.

It may be that a friendly SAARC country with Commonwealth connections is about to become a hostile LDC with a Pakistan connection.

In which case, all will be well.

R.M.

SCHEDULE FOR THE OFFICIAL VISIT OF THE PRESIDENT OF CHAGOS

14.00   The President disembarks, and is met by the Prime Minister.

14.07   National Anthems:
Jana Gana Mana:
52 seconds
Chagos anthem:
3 minutes 25 seconds approx.

14.11   The Prime Minister and the President inspect the Guard of Honour.

14.15   Speech of welcome by the Prime Minister.

14.18   Brief reply by the President.

14.30   Proceed to cars, thence to Raj Bhavan.

15.00   Arrive Raj Bhavan.

[Presumably by 'all will be well' Shri Mathur was referring to the possible cancellation of the official visit, rather than another country joining the Pakistani camp —Ed.]

November 14th

Long lapse since I made any entries in the diary. Partly due to the weekend, which was taken up with boring constituency business. And partly due to pressure of work—boring ministerial business.

I feel that work is being kept from me. Not that I'm short of work. My files are full of irrelevant and unimportant rubbish.

Yesterday I really had nothing to do at all in the afternoon. No engagements of any sort. Kaul was forced to advise me to go to the Lok Sabha and listen to the debate there. I've never heard such a ridiculous suggestion.

Late this afternoon I was in the office, going over the plans for the Chagos visit, and I switched on the TV news. To my horror they reported a coup in Chagos. Marxist, they think. They reported widespread international interest and concern because of Chagos's oil reserves. It seems that the Commander-in-Chief of the Armed Forces, who rejoices in the name of Colonel Salim Mohammed, has been declared President. Or has declared himself President, more likely. And no one knows what has happened to the former President.

I was appalled. Kaul was with me, and I told him to get me the Extenal Affairs Minister at once.

'Shall we scramble?' he said.

'Where to?' I said, then felt rather foolish as I realized what he was talking about. Then I realized it was another of Kaul's daft suggestions: what's the point of using a secure line for a phone conversation about something that's just been on the television news?

I got through to Nair at the Foreign Ministry.

Incredibly, he knew nothing about the coup in Chagos.

'How do you know?' he asked when I told him.

'It's on TV. Didn't you know? You're the Foreign and External Affairs Minister, Nairsaheb.'

'Yes,' said Nair, 'but my TV set's broken.'

I could hardly believe my ears. 'Your TV set? Don't you get the Foreign Ministry telegrams through diplomatic channels?'

Nair said, 'Yes, but they don't come in till much later. A couple of days, maybe. I always get the foreign news from the TV.'

I thought he was joking. It seems he was not. I said that we must make sure that the official visit was still on, come what may. There are three by-elections hanging on it. He agreed.

I rang off, but not before telling Nair to let me know if he heard any more details.

'No, you let *me* know,' Nair said. 'You're the one with the TV set.'

November 15th
Meeting with Mathur first thing this morning. He was very jovial, beaming almost from ear to ear.

'You've heard the sad news about the BBD, Mantriji?' he began, smiling broadly. I nodded.

'It's just a slight inconvenience,' he went on, and made a rotary gesture with both hands. 'The wheels are in motion, it's really quite simple to cancel the arrangements for the visit.'

'You'll do no such thing,' I told him.

'But Mantriji, we have no choice.'

'We do,' I countered. 'I've spoken to the Foreign Minister

already.' His face seemed to twitch a bit. 'We are reissuing the invitation to the new President.'

'New President?' Mathur was aghast. 'But we haven't even recognized his government.'

I made the same rotary gesture with my hands. 'The wheels are in motion,' I smiled. I was enjoying myself at last.

Mathur said, 'We don't know who he is.'

'Somebody Mohammed,' I said.

'But . . . we don't know anything about him. What's he like?'

I pointed out, rather wittily I thought, that we weren't considering him for membership to our exclusive golf club. I said that I didn't give a damn what he was like.

Mathur tried to get tough. 'Mantriji,' he began, 'there is total confusion in Chagos. We don't know who is behind him. We don't know if he has foreign backing, or is just an ordinary Chagoan who's gone berserk. We cannot take diplomatic risks.'

'The government has no choice,' I said.

Mathur tried a new tack. 'We have not done the paperwork.' I ignored this rubbish. Paperwork is the religion of the Administrative Service. I can just imagine Mathur on his deathbed, surrounded by wills and insurance claim forms, looking up and saying, 'I cannot go yet, Bhagvan, I haven't done the paperwork.'

Mathur pressed on. 'The PMO insists that the PM be properly briefed. This is not possible without the paperwork.'

I stood up. 'The PM will cope. He always does.' Now I had put him in the position of having to criticize the PM.

He handled it well. He stood up too. 'Out of the question,' he replied. 'Who *is* he? He might not be properly brought up. He might be rude to him. He might . . . insult him!' The mind boggles. 'And he is bound to be photographed with the PM—what if he then turns out to be another Saddam Hussain? The repercussions are too hideous to contemplate.'

I must say the last point does slightly worry me. But not as much as throwing away three marginals. I spelt out the contrary arguments to Mathur. 'There are reasons of State,' I said, 'which make this visit essential. Chagos is potentially enormously rich. It needs oil drills. We have idle equipment in the North-East. Moreover, it is strategically vital to the government's Chagos policy.'

'The government hasn't got a Chagos policy,' observed Mathur.

'It does now,' I snapped. 'And if the new President is Marxist-backed, who better to win him over to our side than the PM? Furthermore, the people of the North-Eastern States have been promised an important State occasion and we cannot go back on our word.'

'Not to mention,' added Mathur drily, 'three by-elections in marginal constituencies.'

'That has nothing to do with it,' I said, and glowered at him. He said, 'Of course not, Mantriji,' but I'm not quite sure that he believed me.

Then the phone rang. Kaul took the call. It was from the MEA.

Kaul listened, then told us that the new President of Chagos had announced his intention to visit India next week, in line with his predecessor's arrangements.

I was impressed. The MEA was getting the news at last. I asked Kaul if the cables had been repaired. 'Not exactly,' he said. 'The External Affairs Mantriji's driver heard a news flash on his car radio.'

The upshot is that it would now be up to the PM to cancel the visit on my recommendation or Nair's. And I have decided it is on. Another policy decision. Quite a lot of them after all. Good.

November 21st
Today was the first day of the long-awaited official visit. President Mohammed's arrival was shown on TV. Kaul and I were watching in the office—I must admit I was slightly on tenterhooks in case he did turn out to be a bit uncouth.

A jumbo jet touched down, with CHAGOS AIRWAYS written on the side. I was hugely impressed. Air-India are having to pawn their Boeings, and here is this tiny State with its own airline, jumbo jets and all.

I asked Kaul how many planes Chagos Airways had. 'None,' he said.

I told him not to be silly and use his eyes. 'No Mantriji, it belongs to several BBDs,' he said. 'They chartered it and repaint it specially.' Apparently most of the Have-Nots (I mean, LDCs) do this—at the opening of the UN General Assembly the runways of Kennedy Airport are jam-packed with phony flag-carriers. 'In fact,' added Kaul with a sly grin, 'there was one 747 that belonged to nine different African airlines in one month. They called it the mumbo-jumbo.'

'You mean the BBD-ATP? You know, the *boond-barabar deshon ka* air-taxi pool,' I explained to Kaul grandly, feeling very witty.

While we watched nothing much happened on the TV except the BBD-ATP taxiing around the airport and the PM looking a bit chilly. Kaul gave me the day's schedule and explained that I was booked on the night flight from Delhi to Guwahati. Then

149

the commentator, in that special hushed television voice used for any occasion with which the PM is connected, announced reverentially that we were about to catch our first glimpse of President Salim.

And out of the plane stepped George. My old friend George Weight. We were at Gwalior University together. Not Salim Mohammed at all, but George.

Kaul asked me if I were sure. Silly question. How could you forget a name like George Weight?

I sent Kaul to look for Mathur, who was delighted to hear that we now knew something about our official visitor.

Kaul's official brief said nothing. Amazing! Amazing how little the External Affairs Ministry has been able to find out. Perhaps they were hoping it would all be on the car radio. All the brief says is that Colonel Salim Mohammed was converted to Islam some years ago, they didn't know his original name, and therefore knew little of his background.

I was able to tell Mathur and Kaul *all* about his background. George was on the student-exchange programme, NRI-FG, Non-Resident Indian Fifth Generation. He was a red-hot political economist, I informed them. Got the top first. Same department as me, same college, same hostel . . . same Madhu . . .

'Madhu?' asked Kaul and Mathur together.

'A girl in our class, she had blue eyes . . .'

Kaul seemed relieved. 'Well, that's all right then.'

'Why?' I enquired.

'I think Kaul means,' said Mathur helpfully, 'that he'll know how to behave if he was at an Indian University. Even if it was Gwalior.' I never know whether or not Mathur is insulting me intentionally.

Mathur was concerned about George's political colour. 'When

you said he was red-hot, were you speaking politically?'

In a way I was. 'The thing about George is that you never quite know where you are with him. He's the sort of *dal-badlu* fellow who says one thing and does another.' [*Dal-badlu is an inconsistent person, opportunistic, who changes parties frequently for personal gain, commonly known as 'defectors' in Indian political speak, and very common in Indian politics —Ed.*]

'No deeply held convictions?' asked Mathur.

'No. The only thing George was deeply committed to was himself.'

'Ah, I see. A true *neta*, Mantriji. [*Neta means leader (positive connotation) and also politician (negative connotation) in Hindi. Here almost certainly used in the negative sense —Ed.*]

This was definitely one of Mathur's little jokes. He'd never be so rude otherwise. Though sometimes I suspect that Mathur says things he really means and excuses himself by saying 'only joking'. Nonetheless, I was able to put him down by patronizing him with his own inimitable phrase. 'Very charming, Mathursaheb,' I said cuttingly. And I pointed out that as George was only here for three days he couldn't do much harm anyway.

Mathur still seemed concerned. 'Just remember, Mantriji,' he said, 'you wanted him here, not me.'

'If you'll excuse me, Mathursaheb, I must get on with my files,' I said, trying to hide my irritation.

'Just before you do, Mantriji,' said Mathur, 'I'd be most grateful if you would glance at this brief on regional politics.' He handed me a very bulky file. More paper. I declined to read it.

'No thanks,' I said. 'I think I'm all right on all that.'

'Oh good,' he said cheerfully, 'because one wouldn't want to upset the delicate power balance between FROLINAT and

FRETELIN, would one?'

I think he could see that he had got me there. So he pressed home his advantage. 'I mean, if the new President is more sympathetic to ZIPRA than ZANLA, not to mention ZAPU and ZANU, then CARECOM and COREPER might want to bring in GRAPO, and of course that would mean going back over all that old business with ECOSOC and UNIDO and then the whole IBRD–OECD row could blow up again . . . and what would the PMO do if that happened?'

[*FROLINAT was the National Liberation Front of Chad, a French acronym. FRETELIN was the Trust for the Liberation of Timor, a small Portuguese colony seized by Indonesia: a Portuguese acronym. ZIPRA was the Zimbabwe People's Revolutionary Army, ZANLA the Zimbabwe African Liberation Army, ZAPU the Zimbabwe African People's Union, ZANU the Zimbabwe African National Union. CARECOM was the acronym for the Caribbean Common Market and COREPER the Committee of Permanent Representatives to the European Community—a French acronym, pronounced co-ray-pair. ECOSOC was the Economic and Social Council of the UN, UNIDO the United Nations Industrial Development Organization, IBRD the International Bank for Reconstruction and Development and OECD was the Organization for Economic Co-operation and Development. GRAPO could not conceivably have been relevant to the conversation, as it was the Spanish acronym for the First of October Anti-Fascist Revolutionary Group.*

It is not impossible that Shri Mathur may have been trying to confuse his Minister.—Ed.]

The only initials I understood in that whole thing were PMO [*Prime Minister's Office —Ed.*]. As Mathur had predicted, I said—

as casually as I could—that I might as well glance through the file.

'I'll see you on the plane,' he said, and departed smoothly. I'm afraid he won a small moral victory there.

Kaul then tried to hurry me along to the Parliamentary Advisory Committee meeting. But the huge pile of correspondence in my in-tray was now multiplying horrifyingly and apparently reproducing itself. 'What about all this,' I said helplessly. 'What can I do?'

'Well, Mantriji . . .' began Kaul, and his eyes flickered almost imperceptibly across to the out-tray a couple of times. I realized that I had very little choice. I picked up the whole pile of letters and moved them solemnly from the in-tray to the out-tray.

It was a funny feeling. I felt both guilty and relieved. Kaul seemed to think I had done the right thing. The inevitable thing, perhaps. '*Shabaash*, Mantriji,' he said in a kindly tone, 'better out than in.' [*Shabaash—well done! —Ed.*]

November 22nd

Last night was a horrendous experience, one that I do not intend to repeat in a hurry.

And today a massive crisis has yet to be solved. And it's all my fault. And I don't know if I can carry it off. Oh God!

To begin at the beginning. I was off to my meeting in South Block and was waiting at the lift. These lifts are slower than the Administrative Service. Suddenly, a panic-stricken Kaul came running towards me.

'Kaul, what is it *bhai*?' I asked.

He was breathless and sweating. I had never seen him in such a state. Come to think of it, I've never seen any civil servant in such a state. They all seem so frightfully calm and controlled most of the time, in a funny way it's rather reassuring to see that they sometimes panic just like the rest of the human race, and that when they do they just run around like headless chickens.

Kaul was clutching a long roll of fax paper.

'Read this, Mantriji,' he said dramatically, and thrust the fax at my chest.

I was thoroughly irritated. Kaul is endlessly pushing paper at me. I already had four files in my bag.

I thrust the fax back at him. 'I will read it later,' I said.

'You must read it now, Mantriji,' he said, and back it came as though we were playing pass the parcel. 'This is top priority.'

'You always say that about everything,' I pointed out. By this time, I had missed the lift.

Kaul informed me that he was offering me an advance copy of President Salim's speech for tomorrow (today now—oh my *God*!) which had been sent around by the Chagoan Embassy.

I wasn't interested. These speeches are always the same: happy to be here, thanks for the gracious welcome, ties between our two countries, bonds of shared experience, happy and fruitful cooperation in the future, and all the usual nonsense.

Kaul agreed that all of that rubbish was in the speech, but insisted that I read the important bits at once—bits he had underlined in red ink. He then said he was distributing it to the others—Mathur and the Secretary to the MEA and our press officer and assorted other dignitaries.

I opened the envelope as I got into the lift and saw the most appalling sight. A speech that we *cannot* allow to be delivered.

> *mantriji:* The people of Chagos have full sympathy
> *your views* for oppressed people all over the world,
> particularly of the North and the North-
> *urgently.* East of India. In Chagos we have thrown off
> our chains and we urge our brothers of the
> *Kaul.* Bodo and ULFA movements to liberate
> themselves from the oppression of the Indian

I stopped the lift and was about to question Kaul, when Mathur stepped into the open lift. I expressed my feelings about the utter disaster that awaited us if this speech was read out in front of the PM.

Mathur replied that he didn't like to say that he had told me so, but he had told me so.

I reiterated that something had to be done. The lift was going up and three by-elections hung in the balance, not counting the effects on other regions! 'This is a catastrophe,' I whispered.

Mathur did not exactly seem to be at pains to minimize the situation. 'It is indeed,' he agreed solemnly, piling on the agony. 'A catastrophe. A tragedy. A cataclysmic, apocalyptic, monumental calamity.' He paused for breath, and then added bluntly, 'And you did it.'

This was not exactly helping. 'Mathursaheb,' I reproached him. 'You're paid to advise me. Advise me!'

'All in all,' replied Mathur, 'this is not unlike trying to advise the captain of the *Titanic* after he has struck the iceberg.'

'Come on,' I said, 'there must be *something* we can do.'

'We could sing "*Ekla Chalo Re*".' ['*I walk alone*'—*a Tagore song*—*Ed.*]

'Mantriji,' Kaul piped up as the lift came back to ground level and the lift doors opened, 'the External Affairs Minister would like a word.'

Nair joined me and Mathur in the lift. 'Welcome to the lift conference, Nairsaheb,' I remarked ironically.

'You've read the speech?' Nair asked.

I asked him why Salim Mohammed would want to make such a speech here. Nair reckoned it was for home consumption, to boost his image in his country that he is a real revolutionary.

Kaul, who had joined us in the lift, suggested that we draft a statement in response to the speech. I thought that was a good idea.

I asked Mathur if a statement was a good idea.

'Well Mantriji,' he replied carefully, 'in practical terms we have, in fact, the usual six options. One, do nothing. Two, issue a statement deploring the speech. Three, lodge an official protest. Four, cut off aid. Five, break off diplomatic relations. Six, declare war.'

This sounded like rather a lot of options. I was pleased. I asked him which we should do.

'One: if we do nothing we implicitly agree with the speech. Two: if we issue a statement we just look foolish. Three: if we lodge a protest it will be ignored. Four: we can't cut off aid because we don't give them any. Five: if we break off diplomatic relations we cannot negotiate the oil rig contracts. Six: if we declare war it just *might* look as if we were over-reacting.'

I was desperate by this time.

'What do we do about this hideous *speech*?' I asked nervously.

'Well now,' began Nair, 'I think we know what's behind this, don't we Mathur?'

'I think that Nairsaheb is suggesting that the offending paragraph of the speech may be, shall we say, a bargaining counter.'

'A move in the game,' said Nair.

'The first shot in a battle,' said Mathur.

'An opening gambit,' said Kaul.

These civil servants are truly masters of the cliché. They can go on all night. They do, unless stopped. I stopped them.

'You mean, he wants something,' I said incisively. It was lucky someone was on the ball.

'If he doesn't,' enquired Nair, 'why give us a copy in advance?' This seems unarguable. 'But unfortunately the usual channels are blocked because the High Commission staff are all new and we've only just seen the speech. And no one knows anything about this new President.'

I could see Mathur giving me meaningful looks.

'I do,' I volunteered, slightly reluctantly.

Nair looked amazed.

'They were at Gwalior University together,' Mathur said.

Nair turned to me. 'The old-boys' network?' It seemed to be a question.

I wasn't awfully keen on this turn of events. After all, it's twenty-five years since I saw George, he might not remember me, I don't know what I can achieve. 'I think you ought to see him, Nairsaheb; you . . . it will carry a lot of weight,' I replied.

'Singhsaheb, I think you carry as much weight as me,' said Nair.

I realized that I had no choice. 'All right,' I agreed, and turned to Mathur, 'but you're coming with me.'

'Of course,' said Mathur, 'I'd hardly let you do it on your own.'

Is this *another* insult, or is it just my paranoia?

Later today:

George Weight—perhaps I had better call him President Salim from now on—welcomed us to his suite at the hotel at 10 a.m.

'Ah Surya.' He rose to greet us courteously. I had forgotten what beautiful English he spoke. 'Come in, how nice to see you.'

I was actually rather, well, gratified by this warm reception.

'George,' I said. We shook hands. 'Long time no see.'

I introduced Mathur, and we all sat down.

'I've always thought that Secretary is such a demeaning title,' he said. Mathur's eyebrows shot up.

'I beg your pardon?'

'It sounds like an assistant typist or something,' said George pleasantly, and Mathur's eyebrows disappeared into his hairline. 'Whereas,' he continued in the same tone, 'you're really in charge of everything, aren't you?' he said to me. George hasn't changed a bit.

Mathur regained his composure and preened. 'Not quite everything.'

I then congratulated George on becoming Head of State. 'Thank you,' he said, 'though it wasn't difficult. I didn't have to do any of the boring things like fighting elections.' He paused, and then added casually, 'Or by-elections,' and smiled amiably at us.

Was this a hint? I decided to say nothing. So after a moment he went on. 'Surya, of course I'm delighted to see you, but is this purely a social visit or is there anything you particularly wanted to talk about? Because I do have to put the finishing touches to my speech.'

Another hint?

I told him we had seen the advance copy. He asked if we liked it. I asked him if, as we were old friends, I could speak

158

frankly. He nodded.

I tried to make him realize that the bit about the oppression was slightly—well, really, *profoundly* embarrassing. I asked him if he couldn't just snip out the whole chunk about the North-East.

George responded by saying, 'This is something that I feel very deeply to be true. Surely the Indian government doesn't believe in suppressing the truth?'

A neat move.

Mathur then tried to help. 'I wonder if there is anything that might persuade the President to consider recasting the sentence in question so as to transfer the emphasis from the specific instance to the abstract concept, without impairing the conceptual integrity of the theme?'

Some help.

I sipped my coffee with a thoughtful expression on my face.

Even George hadn't got it, I don't think, because he said, after quite a pause, 'While you're here, Surya, may I sound you out on a proposal I was going to make to the Prime Minister at our talks?'

I nodded.

He then told us that his little change of government in Chagos had alarmed some of the investors in their oil industry. Quite unnecessarily, in his view. So he wants some investment from India to tide him over.

At last we were talking some *matlab ki baat* [*Hindi phrase to mean 'talking turkey' —Ed.*].

I asked how much. He said five hundred crores.

Mathur looked concerned. He wrote me a little note. 'Ask him on what terms.' So I asked.

'Repayment of the capital not to start before ten years. And interest free.'

It sounded all right to me, but Mathur choked into his coffee. So I pointed out that five hundred crores was a lot of money.

'Oh well, in that case . . .' began George, and I could see that he was about to end the meeting.

'But let's talk about it,' I calmed him down. I got another note from Mathur, which pointed out that, if interest ran at ten per cent on average, and if the loan was interest free for ten years, he was in effect asking for a free gift of five hundred crores.

Cautiously, I put this point to George. He very reasonably (I thought) explained that it was all to our advantage, because they would use the loan to buy oil drilling equipment from India.

I could see the truth of this, but I got another frantic and, by now, almost illegible note from Mathur, saying that George wanted us to give him five hundred crores so that *he* can buy *our* oil rigs with *our* money. (His underlinings, I may say.)

We couldn't go on passing notes to each other like naughty schoolboys, so we progressed to muttering. 'It sounds pretty reasonable to me,' I whispered.

'You can't be serious,' Mathur hissed.

'Lots of jobs,' I countered, and I asked George, if we did such a deal, would he make appropriate cuts in his speech? This was now cards on the table.

George feigned surprise at my making this connection, but agreed that he would make cuts. However, he'd have to know right away.

'Blackmail,' Mathur had progressed to a stage whisper that could be heard right across the room.

'Are you referring to me or to my proposal?' asked George.

'Your proposal, naturally,' I said hastily and then realized this was a trick question. 'No, not even your proposal.'

I turned to Mathur, and said that I thought we could agree to this. After all, there are precedents for this type of deal. [*Suryaprakash might perhaps have been thinking of the Malaysian shipbuilding deal during the 1970s, by which India lent money interest free to the Malaysians, so that they could buy oil tankers from India with Indian money, tankers which were then going to compete against India's own shipping industry. These tankers were to be built in Kerala, a state with high unemployment. It could have been said that the government was using public money to buy votes, but no one did—perhaps because, like germ warfare, no one wants to risk using an uncontrollable weapon that may in due course be used against oneself.—Ed.*]

Mathur demanded a private word with me, so we went and stood in the corridor. I couldn't see why Mathur was so steamed up. George had offered us a way out.

Mathur said we'd never get the money back, and therefore he could not recommend it to the Finance Ministry and the Finance Ministry would never recommend it to Cabinet. 'You are proposing,' he declared pompously, 'to buy your way out of a political entanglement with five hundred crores of public money.'

I explained that this is diplomacy. He said it was corruption. I said 'Padma Shree,' only just audibly.

There was a long pause.

'What did you say, Mantriji?'

'Nothing,' I said.

Mathur suddenly looked extremely thoughtful. 'On the other hand . . .' he said, '. . . we don't want the Pakistanis to invest in Chagos, do we?' I shook my head. 'Yes, I see what you mean,' he murmured.

'And they will if we don't,' I said, helping him along a bit. Mathur started to marshal all the arguments on my side. 'I suppose we could argue that we, as a part of the North–South dialogue, have a responsibility to the . . .'

'BBDs?' I said.

Mathur ignored the crack. 'Quite,' he said. 'And if we were to insist on one per cent of the equity in the oil revenues ten years from now . . . yes, on balance, I think we can draft a persuasive case in terms of our Third-World obligations, to bring in the External Affairs Ministry . . . and backward area employment, that should carry with us both the Ministry of Employment and the North-Eastern state governments . . . then the oil rig construction should mobilize the Ministry of Trade and Industry, and if we can reassure the Finance Ministry that the balance of payments wouldn't suffer . . . Yes, I think we might be able to get a consensus on this.'

I thought he would come to that conclusion. We trooped back into George's room.

'Mr President,' said Mathur, 'I think we can come to terms with each other after all.'

'You know my price,' said George.

'And you know mine,' I said. I smiled at Mathur. 'Everyone has his price, haven't they?'

Mathur looked inscrutable again.

'Ji Mantriji,' he replied.

6

Raaz Ki Baat
(The Writing on the Wall)

November 27th

The help that I received from Sushilji in the matter of the National Data Base [*see Chapter 3 —Ed.*] might seem unusual to those who are outside the extraordinary world of politics. Strange though it may seem to those members of the public who read numerous abusive speeches in which members of rival political parties revile each other as incompetent, dishonest, criminally stupid and negligent, cross-party friendships are extremely common. In fact, it is much easier to be friends with a member of the opposite party than a member of one's own party—for one is not in direct personal competition for office with members of the Opposition in the way that one is with one's colleagues.

All my Cabinet colleagues and I were naturally in bitter competition with each other during our years in Opposition. In the last three months we've all been so busy trying to deal with the *real* opposition—the Administrative Service—that we've not had any real time to do-down each other. But I have a hunch, from the recent atmosphere in Cabinet, that some political manoeuvring is in the air again.

There are still numerous other matters concerning me, about which I have also had a little time to reflect this weekend. I realized early on (in my first week as a Minister, in fact) that the idea of *Khuli Sarkar* presents real problems. It was made clear to me that if people stop having secrets they stop having power.

In fact, paradoxically, government is more open when it is less open. Open Government is rather like the live theatre: the audience gets a performance. And it gives a response. But, like the theatre, in order to have something to show openly there must first be much hidden activity. And all sorts of things have to be cut or altered in rehearsals, and not shown to the public until you have got them right.

The drawback with all this is that it begs the question—which is that the Administrative Service keeps secrets from Ministers. They say they don't, but I'm sure they do. I'm now all in favour of keeping secrets from the public of course, for the reasons I've just given, but it should be *my* privilege, as the people's elected representative, to decide when to keep the people in ignorance. It should not be up to the Administrative Service to keep *me* in ignorance.

Unfortunately, it is pretty hard to get this across to them.

I have also learned a few general lessons. I must never show my hopes or fears to Mathur, if I can avoid it—especially party fears. If you give away your political weaknesses, they'll destroy you. You have to keep them guessing.

I now realize that I should always get civil servants to commit themselves first. Never say, 'I think . . .', but always say, 'What do *you* think . . .?'

I've also learned about 'yes' and 'no'. You can always turn a 'no' into a 'yes'—but not vice versa. Furthermore, when you say 'no', let the Private Office say it for you—but when you say 'yes', pre-empt the Private Office and phone up yourself. That way, *they* get the blame and *I* get the credit.

In fact, the point about making your own phone calls is crucial. The whole system is designed to prevent you from doing anything yourself. As far as the Administrative Service is concerned, you must never make a phone call, or sort out a problem. Woe betide any Mantri who lifts the phone to try to sort out a foreign trade deal, for instance. Civil servants will come at you from all sides mouthing phrases like, 'it's an External Affairs matter . . . correct channels . . . policy hangs by a thread . . . you *do* realize, don't you? . . . what if something were to go wrong? . . . on your head be it, Mantriji!' and many others.

This is all very squashing to the morale of an important public figure such as myself. If you're not careful they'll eventually have you in such a state that you'll be frightened to phone a restaurant.

Furthermore, everything that one does is carefully watched and supervised. Kaul listens in to all my phone calls, except the ones that I make on the private line. The theory is that he can make useful notes on my behalf, and is fully informed about my views and activities—true! But, as we know, information is a double-edged sword. [*It's no accident that most of the really powerful offices in the world are called 'Secretary'—Secretary of State, Permanent Secretary, General Secretary, Party Secretary, etc. 'Secretary' means the person who is entrusted with secrets, the information no one else knows—the elite. —Ed.*]

I must say, though, that I find it an invaluable way to pass on criticism of my permanent officials, knowing that Kaul is listening in to my every word!

Tonight, in one of my files, there is a third redraft of a report to the Cabinet committee on Administrative Service overmanning. I'm still not pleased with it. I shall have a lot of questions to ask about it tomorrow morning.

November 28th

We had a meeting about the Cabinet committee report. I told Mathur that I still wasn't happy with it, and he obligingly offered to redraft it.

This hardly seemed to be the answer. I pointed out that he had redrafted it three times already.

Kaul argued about this. 'That's not quite correct, Mantriji.' I told him I could count. And that this was the third draft. 'Quite so,' he said. 'It has been drafted once and redrafted twice.' A typical piece of boring pedantic quibbling. Kaul has an idiotic obsession about using language with accuracy—it's fortunate he's not in politics.

I told him not to quibble, and Mathur said placatingly that he would be happy to redraft the report a third time. Of course he would. And a fourth time, and a fifth no doubt. 'And a sixth,' I went on. 'But it still won't say what I want it to say, it will say what *you* want it to say. And I want it to say what *I* want it to say.'

'What do you want it to say?' asked Kaul.

'We want it to say what *you* want it to say,' murmured Mathur soothingly.

'I'm sure,' wittered Kaul, 'that the Department doesn't want you to say something that you don't want to say.'

I tried again. For the fourth time in as many weeks I explained the position. 'Six weeks ago the Cabinet committee asked for our evidence on Administrative Service overmanning. Three times I have briefed a group of civil servants in words of one syllable— and each time I get back a totally unintelligible draft which says the exact opposite of what I have told them to say.'

'With respect, Mantriji,' countered Mathur (untruthfully), 'how do you know it says the opposite if it is totally unintelligible?' He really is the master of the irrelevant-question-begging-answer.

'All I want to say,' I explained plaintively, 'is that the Administrative Service is grossly overmanned and must be slimmed down.'

'I'm sure we all want to say that,' lied my Secretary. 'And that is what the report says.'

'No it doesn't.'

'Yes it does.'

Then we said, 'Oh no, it doesn't,' 'Oh yes, it does,' 'Oh no, it doesn't,' at each other for a while. Then I quoted phrases from the draft report at him. It says, for instance, that a phased reduction of about a hundred thousand people is 'not in the public interest'. Translation: it *is* in the public interest but it is not in the interest of the Administrative Service. 'Public opinion is not yet ready for such a step,' it says. Translation: public opinion is ready but the Administrative Service is not! Then it goes on: 'However, this is an urgent problem and we therefore propose setting up a Justice Commission.' Translation: this problem is a bloody nuisance, but we hope that by the time a Justice Commission reports, four years from now, everyone will have forgotten about it or we can find someone else to blame. *[Suryaprakash was beginning to understand Administrative Service code language. Other examples are:*

'I think we have to be very careful.' Translation: We are not going to do this.

'Have you thought through all the implications?' Translation: You are not going to do this.

'It is a slightly puzzling decision.' Translation: Idiotic!

'Not entirely straightforward.' Translation: Criminal.

'With the greatest possible respect, Mantriji . . .' Translation: Mantriji, that is the silliest idea I've ever heard. —Ed.]

Mathur could see no way out of this impasse. 'Mantriji, I can only suggest that we redraft it.' Brilliant!

'Mathursaheb,' I said, 'will you give me a straight answer to a straight question?'

This question took him completely by surprise, and he stopped to think for a brief moment.

'So long as you are not asking me to resort to crude generalizations or vulgar over-simplifications, such as a simple yes or no,' he said, in a manner that contrived to be both openly ingenuous and deeply evasive, 'I shall do my utmost to oblige.'

'Do you mean yes?' I asked.

A fierce internal struggle appeared to be raging within. 'Yes,' he said finally.

'Right,' I said. 'Here is the straight question.'

Mathur's face fell. 'Oh,' he said, 'I thought that was it.'

I persevered. 'Mathursaheb, in your evidence to the Cabinet committee, are you going to support my view that the Administrative Service is overmanned and feather-bedded or not? Yes or no! Straight answer!'

Could I have put this question any more plainly? I don't think so. This was the reply: 'Mantriji, if I am pressed for a straight answer I shall say that, as far as we can see, looking at it by and large, taking one thing with another, in terms of the average of departments, then in the last analysis it is probably true to say that, at the end of the day, you would find, in general terms that, not to put too fine a point on it, there really was not very much in it one way or the other.'

While I was still reeling from this, he added, no doubt for further clarification, 'As far as one can see, at this stage.'

I made one last attempt. 'Does that mean yes or no?' I asked, without much hope.

'Yes and no,' he replied helpfully.

'Suppose,' I said, 'suppose you *weren't* asked for a straight answer?'

'Ah,' he said happily, 'then I should play for time, Mantriji.'

Mathur's never going to change. I certainly will never change him. Today I got nowhere fast. No, not even fast—I got nowhere, slowly and painfully! The conversation finished with Mathur suggesting that I take the draft home and study it for the next couple of days, because I might then find that it does indeed say what I want it to say. An idiotic time-wasting suggestion, of course. He's just trying to wear me down.

'And if it doesn't say what I want it to say?' I asked testily.

Mathur smiled. 'Then we shall be happy to redraft it for you, Mantriji,' he said.

Back to square one.

November 29th

I have thought about yesterday's events very carefully. I do not propose to give this draft back to the Department for any more redrafting. I shall write it myself, and not return it until it is too late for them to change it.

I mentioned this to Kaul, and he thought it was a good idea. I told him in the strictest confidence, and I hope I can trust him. I'm sure I can.

[*Suryaprakash reckoned without the pressures that the Administrative Service can apply to its own people. Shri Mathur enquired about the fourth draft report several times over the next two weeks, and observed that Shri Kaul was giving evasive answers. Finally, Kaul was invited for a disciplinary drink at Shri Mathur's club in Delhi. We have found a memo about the meeting among Shri Mathur's private papers. —Ed.*]

Kaul came for a drink at the Club.
I questioned him about the Department's Report to the Cabinet committee.

Kaul came for a drink at the Club.

I questioned him about the Department's Report to the

Cabinet committee. He said, 'You mean, Mantriji's report?' A not-insignificant remark.

In answer to my questions as to why we had not yet had it returned to us, he suggested that I ask Mantriji. A most unsatisfactory reply.

I explained that I had chosen to ask *him*. As he remained stubbornly silent, I observed that he did not seem to be replying.

'Yes and no,' he said. He knows full well that this is one of my favourite replies, and I felt obliged to tick him off for impertinence.

In answer to other questions, Kaul insisted that Mantriji is doing his files conscientiously, but repeatedly refused to explain the delay over the draft report, merely advising me to enquire of Mantriji himself as he (Kaul) was Mantriji's *Private* Secretary.

He appeared to be anxious about his situation, and clearly had been put under some obligation by Mantriji to treat some piece of information in strict confidence. I therefore decided to increase his anxiety considerably, to the extent that he would be obliged to find a way of either satisfying both myself and his Mantri, and therefore showing that he is worthy to be a flyer or of taking one side or the other, thereby revealing an inability to walk a tightrope in a high wind.

I therefore reminded him that he was an employee of the IAS. And, admirable though it is to be loyal to his Mantri, an average Mantri's tenure is a mere eleven months whereas Kaul's career will, one hopes, last until the age of sixty.

Kaul handled the situation with skill. He opted for asking me a hypothetical question, always a good idea.

He asked me: *if* a purely hypothetical Mantri were to be unhappy with a Departmental draft of evidence to a committee, and *if* the hypothetical Mantri were to be planning to replace it with his own hypothetical draft worked out with his own political advisers at his party HO, and *if* this Mantri was planning to bring in his own draft so close to the final date for evidence that there would be no time to redraft it, and *if* the hypothetical Private Secretary in question were to be aware of this hypothetical draft—in confidence—should the hypothetical Private Secretary pass on the information to the Secretary of the hypothetical Department?

A good question. Naturally, I answered Kaul by saying that no Private Secretary should pass on such information, if given in confidence.

Kaul shows more promise than I thought.

[*Mathur Papers* 23 /RPY /1 3c]

December 11th

It is now two weeks since I decided to take over the Central Policy Staff Review report. My final redraft is going well. Dikshit and his chaps have been hard at work on it, and I've been burning the midnight oil as well. The situation seems to be infuriating Mathur, which gives me considerable pleasure.

Today he again asked me about my redraft of the redraft of the draft. 'What about the evidence to the Central Policy Review Staff?' he said.

'You mean the report?' I said playing for time.

'Ji Mantriji.'

'Why do you want it?' I asked.

'So that we can redraft it.'

'That won't be necessary.'

'I think it will, Mantriji.'

'Mathursaheb,' I said firmly, 'drafting is not an Administrative Service monopoly.'

'It is a highly specialized skill,' he replied, 'which few people outside the Service can master.'

'Nonsense,' I said. 'Drafts are easy. It's a game anyone can play.'

'Not without losing,' he answered. Actually, he's quite witty, really.

I chuckled at his joke, and changed the subject. But he didn't let me get away with it.

'So can I have the draft back, please?' he persisted.

'Of course,' I said, with a smile. He waited. In vain.

'When, Mantriji?' he asked, trying to smile back, but definitely through clenched teeth.

'Later,' I said airily.

'But *when*?' he snarled through his smile.

'You always say we mustn't rush things,' I said irritatingly.

He then asked me for a straight answer! The nerve of it! However, as he had started to use my terminology, I answered him in his.

'In due course, Mathursaheb.' I was really enjoying myself. 'In the fullness of time. At the appropriate juncture. When the moment is ripe. When the requisite procedures have been completed. Nothing precipitate, you understand.'

'Mantriji,' he said, losing all traces of good humour. 'It is getting urgent.'

He was getting rattled. Great. My tactics were a triumph. 'Urgent?' I said blandly. 'You *are* learning a lot of new words.' I don't think I've ever been quite so rude to anyone in my life. I was having a wonderful time. I must try it more often.

'I hope you will forgive me for saying this,' began Mathur in his iciest manner, 'but I am beginning to suspect that you are concealing something from me.'

I feigned shock, surprise, puzzlement, ignorance—a whole

mass of false emotions. 'Mathursaheb!' I said in my most deeply shocked voice. 'Surely we don't have any secrets from each other?'

'I'm sorry, Mantriji, but sometimes one is forced to consider the possibility that affairs are being conducted in a way which, all things being considered, and making all possible allowances, is, not to put too fine a point on it, perhaps not entirely straightforward.' Mathur was insulting me in the plainest language he could manage in a crisis. Not entirely straightforward, indeed!

So I decided to come clean at last. I told him that I have redrafted the redraft myself, that I'm perfectly happy with it, and that I don't want him to redraft it again.

'But . . .' began Mathur.

'No buts,' I snapped. 'All I get from the Administrative Service is delaying tactics.'

'I wouldn't call Administrative Service delays "tactics", Mantriji,' he replied smoothly. 'That would be to mistake lethargy for strategy.'

I asked him if we hadn't already set up a committee to investigate delays in the Administrative Service. He concurred.

'What happened to it?' I asked.

'Oh,' he said, brushing the matter aside, 'it hasn't met yet.'

'Why not?' I wanted to know.

'There . . . seems to have been a delay,' he admitted.

It is vital that I make Mathur realize that there is a real desire for radical reform in the air. I reminded him that the All-Party Select Committee on Administrative Affairs, which I founded, has been a great success.

This was probably an error, because he immediately asked me what it has achieved. I was forced to admit that it hasn't actually achieved anything *yet*, but I pointed out that the party is very pleased by it.

'Really?' he asked. 'Why?'

'Ten column inches in the *Business Standard* last Monday, for a start,' I replied proudly.

'I see,' he said coldly, 'the government is to measure its success in column inches, is it?'

'Yes . . . and no,' I said with a smile.

But he was deeply concerned about my redraft of the draft report. 'Mantriji,' he said firmly, 'the evidence that you are proposing to submit is not only untrue, it is—which is much more serious—unwise.' One of Mathur's most telling remarks so far, I think. 'We have been through this before: the expanding Administrative Service is the result of Parliamentary legislation, not bureaucratic empire building.'

I began to think that Mathur really believes this.

'So,' I said, 'when this comes up on Question Time you want me to tell Parliament it's their fault that the Administrative Service is so big?'

'It's the truth, Mantriji,' he insisted. He can't seem to grasp that I don't want the truth, I want something I can tell Parliament.

I spelled it out to him. 'Mathursaheb, you are my Secretary. Are you going to support me?'

'We shall always support you as your standard-bearers, Mantriji—but not as your pall-bearers.'

There seemed to be a vaguely threatening air about these remarks. I demanded to know what he was actually *saying*. As I was becoming more and more heated, he was becoming icier and icier.

'I should have thought,' he pronounced, in his most brittle voice with excessive clarity of enunciation, 'that my meaning was crystal-clear. Do not give such a report to a body whose

176

recommendations are to be published.'

As always, he had completely missed the point. I explained that it was *because* the report is to be published that I was submitting the evidence. *I,* the Minister, am to be the judge of when to keep secrets, *not* the permanent officials.

I appeared to have silenced him completely. Then, after a rather long pause for thought, he enquired if he might make one more suggestion.

'Only if it's in plain English,' I replied.

'If you must do this damn silly thing,' he said, 'don't do it in this damn silly way.'

December 12th

On the way to PMO this morning Kaul showed me the agenda for Cabinet. To my horror, I was informed that Cabinet was due to discuss my proposal to close down the Land Registry—or what was *described* as my proposal! I had never heard of it till that moment. It is a scheme to transfer residual functions to the Property Services Agency. The idea is to reduce the number of autonomous government departments. Kaul told me I had initialled it. God knows when—I suppose it must have been in a file sometime over the last few weeks but I don't recall it. I had been working on the report and nothing else for the last week or more. Anyway, I can't remember every paper I struggle through at one or two a.m.—in fact, I can hardly remember any of them. There has to be a better system than this.

Mathur assured me that I didn't really need to know much about the proposal because his information on the grapevine, through the Private Office network, was that the proposal would go through on the nod.

[Regrettably, this situation was not as uncommon as the reader

might suppose. Because of both the pressure of time and the complexity of much legislation, Ministers frequently had to propose measures to Cabinet that they themselves either had not read or did not fully understand. Hence the distinction sometimes drawn between Ministerial policy, i.e. policies about which the Minister has strong personal views or commitments, and Ministry policy, i.e. most policy. —Ed.]

December 13th

Today was the blackest day so far. Perhaps not only the blackest day since I became a Minister, but the blackest day since I went into politics.

I am deeply depressed.

However, I feel I must record the events of the day, and I'll do so in the order in which they occurred.

It appears that Mathur went to the usual weekly Secretaries' meeting this morning. It seems that he was ticked off by a couple of his colleagues when he revealed that I had written the draft report for the Cabinet committee.

Mathur complained to Kaul about my behaviour, it seems, and Kaul—who seems to be the only one I can totally trust—told me. Apparently Shri Vijay Raman—the Cabinet Secretary—actually said to Mathur that once you allow a Minister to write a draft report, the next thing you know they'll be dictating policy.

Incredible!

It is true, of course. I have learned that he who drafts the document wins the day.

[This is the reason why it was common Administrative Service practice at this time to write the minutes of a meeting before the meeting took place. This achieves two things. First, it helps the Chairman or Secretary to ensure that the discussion follows the

lines agreed on beforehand and that the right points are made by somebody. And second, as busy men generally cannot quite remember what was agreed at meetings, it is extremely useful and convenient to lay it down in advance. Only if the conclusions reached at a meeting are radically different or diametrically opposed to what has been previously written in the minutes will the officials have to rewrite them. Thus it is that pre-written minutes can dictate the results of many meetings, regardless of what may be said or agreed by those actually present. —Ed.]

Mathur and Raman were discussing Mathur's plan *(not* mine, I may add!) for reducing the number of autonomous government departments, when they encountered Raibabu, who overheard their conversation. [*Raibabu was the Prime Minister's Senior Policy Adviser, brought into government from outside. Tough, intelligent, hard-bitten and with no love for senior civil servants. —Ed.*]

Raibabu revealed that the Cabinet committee recommendation accepted the idea of reducing the number of autonomous government departments. This news came as a profound shock to Mathur, because not all the ministerial evidence has been taken—ours, for instance, has not!

However, it seems that they have reported unofficially, and clearly the report is not going to change now, no matter what we say. Raibabu explained to Mathur that the Central Policy Review Staff do not sully their elevated minds with anything as squalid as evidence from ministers!

Mathur, at first, was not unhappy with Raibabu's news. Naturally, as an experienced civil servant, a proposal to reduce and simplify the administration of government conjured up in Mathur's mind a picture of a large intake of new staff specifically to deal with the reductions.

However, this is not the plan at all. Mathur informed me, at an urgently convened meeting at 9 a.m. this morning that Raibabu had made these points:

1 That Suryaprakash Singh is always seeking to reduce overmanning in the Administrative Service.

2 That he is going to succeed, at last.

3 And that to facilitate this matter, the Finance Ministry, the Home Ministry and the UPSC have all proposed abolishing the Ministry of Administrative Affairs.

4 And that 'the PM is smiling on the plan' (his very words).

Appalling! My job's at stake.

It seems that the PM is entranced by the idea, on the grounds that it is neat, clean, dramatic, and will be politically popular.

The plan is that all the MAA's functions will be subsumed by other departments.

And my fate? Apparently it is to be presented to the press and public that I have won through with a public-spirited self-sacrificing policy, and I'm to be kicked upstairs to the Governorship of a small, insignificant territory.

Apparently Raibabu was very pleased with himself, and with this plan, presumably because of his own crusade against Administrative Service extravagance, bureaucracy and waste. Ironically, I agree with him on all that—but not at the expense of *my* job, thank you very much.

This certainly confirms my instincts, that some political Cabinet in-fighting was due to start up again, and clearly we have a huge fight on our hands. Everyone's against us. The Secretaries of the Finance Ministry, Home Ministry and UPSC all stand to gain more power and influence. So do my Cabinet colleagues running those departments. And, of course, I always knew that the MAA was a political graveyard and that the PM might have been handing me a poisoned chalice—after all, I did run a leadership campaign against the PM.

It seems that Raibabu, to do him justice, also pointed out that Mathur would also be on the way out. 'There's a placement agency behind Mohan Singh Place,' he said maliciously. 'Shall I find you the telephone number?'

This is the only remotely amusing thing I've heard in the last twenty-four hours.

So when Mathur brought me up-to-date this morning, I was appalled. I could hardly believe it at first. I told Mathur I was appalled.

'You're appalled?' he said. 'I'm appalled.'

Kaul said he was appalled, too.

And, there's no doubt about it, the situation is appalling.

I have no doubt that the situation is as described by Mathur and Raibabu is true. It rings true. And Mathur, yesterday, saw the Joint Departmental proposal made by the Finance Ministry, Home Ministry and UPSC. And Raibabu is very close to the PM too, so he must know what's going on.

I asked Mathur if I'd get another job, whether or not I was being given a Governorship. And, incidentally, I shall definitely refuse a Padma Shree if it is offered.

'There is a rumour,' replied Mathur gravely, 'of a new post. Minister with general responsibility for Labour Welfare.'

This was the worst news yet. Labour Welfare. That means strikes. From now on, every strike in India will be my fault. Marvellous!

I pondered this for some moments. My reverie was interrupted by Mathur enquiring in a sepulchral tone: 'Have you considered what might happen to *me*, Mantriji? I'll probably be sent to *Pashupalan* [*animal husbandry* —Ed.]. The rest of my career dedicated to arguing about the fisheries quota.'

Kaul dared to smile a little smile, and Mathur turned on him. 'And as for you, young man, if your Mantri bites the dust your reputation as a flyer—such as it is—will be hit for six. You'll probably spend the rest of your career at a shipyard in the Andamans.'

'My God,' said Kaul quietly.

We sat in silence, lost in our own tragic thoughts, for some considerable time. I heaved a sigh. So did Mathur. Then Kaul.

Of course, the whole thing is Mathur's fault. Reducing the number of autonomous government departments was an idiotic proposal, playing right into the hands of our enemies. I said so. He replied that it was all my fault, because of my proposal to the Cabinet committee to carry out the phased reduction of the Administrative Service.

I pooh-poohed this as a ridiculous suggestion because the Cabinet committee hasn't even *seen* our report yet. But Mathur revealed that the party had sent an advance copy to the PM.

So perhaps we've both dropped ourselves in it. Anyway, there was no point in arguing about it, and I asked Mathur for suggestions.

There was another gloomy silence.

'We could put a paper up,' he said finally.

'Up what?' I asked. Brilliant!

Mathur asked me if *I* had any suggestions. I hadn't. We turned to Kaul.

'What do you think, Kaul?'

'I think it's appalling,' he repeated. A lot of use he is.

Then Mathur proposed that we work together on this. This was a novel suggestion, to say the least. I thought his job was to work with me on all occasions. This seemed like an admission.

Furthermore, his idea of our working together is generally that he tells me what to do, and I then do it. And look where it's got us!

However, I asked him what he had to suggest.

'With respect, Mantriji,' he began. This was too much. I told him not to use that insulting language to me ever again! Clearly he was about to imply that anything I had to say on the subject would be beneath contempt.

But Mathur reiterated that he *really* meant that we should work together. 'I need you,' he said.

I must admit I was rather touched. Then, to my utter astonishment, he suggested that we send for Dikshit.

Mathur is clearly a reformed character. Even though it's probably too late to matter!

'You see, Mantriji, if the Prime Minister is behind a scheme, South Block on its own cannot block it. Cabinet Ministers' schemes are easily blocked . . .' he corrected himself at once, '. . . redrafted, but the PM is another matter.'

In a nutshell, his scheme is to fight this plan in Parliament as well as South Block. Therefore he believes that Dikshit can help to mobilize the MPs and splinter groups on my behalf.

I suggested that the papers might be of use, if Dikshit can get the press on our side. Mathur blanched and swallowed, but to his credit agreed. 'If there is no other way, even newspapers . . .' he murmured.

December 14th

Dikshit was away yesterday. So we had the meeting with him today.

He had just heard the news. We asked for his reaction. For the first time that I can remember, he was speechless. He just sat

183

and shook his head sadly. I asked him what suggestions he had.

'I can't think of anything . . . I'm appalled,' he replied. We all agreed that it was appalling.

So I took charge. 'We've got to stop flapping about like wet hens. We've got to do something to save the Ministry from closure. Diskhit, get through to the Whip's office to mobilize MPs and splinter groups, to stop this before it starts.'

'I'm awfully sorry to quibble again, Mantriji, but you can't actually stop things before they start,' intervened Kaul, the wet-hen-in-chief. He's really useless in a crisis.

Dikshit pointed out that this idea of mine wasn't much good, as the scheme to abolish the MAA would probably be popular with MPs. So I pointed out that it was Mathur's idea, anyway.

Kaul's overnight deliberations led him to propose a publicity campaign in the press, full-page ads praising the Ministry. He offered us some slogans: '*Poorey desh ki raksha karta hai administration*' ['*Administration saves the nation*' —*Ed.*] and '*Lal feeta hai jahan usne jeeta hai jahaan*' ['*Whoever has red tape rules the world*'. *Both slogans are parodies of a popular soap commercial.—Ed.*].

We just boggled at these ideas. So he then suggested 'Red Tape Holds the Nation Together'. Sometimes I really despair of Kaul.

There was a long pause, after which Mathur remarked bleakly, 'There's no doubt about it, the writing's on the wall.'

None of us can see any real hope of averting catastrophe. It's appalling!

December 15th
Life must go on, even while the Sword of Damocles hangs over us. Today we had a meeting about the CPSP card scheme *(chota*

parivaar, sukhi parivar—small family, happy family card scheme —Ed). This was a completely new development. I had never even heard of it. Apparently there's been information about it in my files for the last couple of nights, but I've been too depressed and preoccupied to grasp anything I've read.

It seems that the CPSP is a new family planning card, to be carried by all families in the country. All families with more than two children and without a CPSP card will not get any government subsidies—no ration cards etc. And those with CPSPs will get special benefits, reservations, special railway passes etc.

Apparently the PM wants me to introduce the necessary legislation.

I'm *horrified* by this.

Mathur was surprised at my reaction. He thought it was a good idea as I'm a member of the National Population Commission, and he thinks that a CPSP card will help slow down population growth in the long run.

Dikshit and I tried to explain to the officials that for me to introduce such a scheme would be political suicide. The Indian people do not want to carry compulsory identification papers. I'll be accused of trying to bring in a police state, when I'm still not fully recovered from the fuss about the Data Base. 'Is this what we fought for in the Independence Movement?' I can hear the MPs cry.

'But it's nothing more than a sort of identity card,' said Mathur.

'It's the last nail in my coffin,' said I.

Dikshit asked why we had to introduce it, not the Health fellows? A good question.

'I understand,' explained Mathur, 'that the PM did originally suggest that the Ministry for Health introduce the measure, but the Secretary of the Ministry for Health suggested that it was a Social Welfare measure, and then the Home Ministry took the view that it is essentially an administrative matter. The PM agreed.'

Dikshit said, 'They're all playing pass the parcel.'

Can you blame them, when they can hear it ticking?

Mathur then observed mournfully that the identity card bill would probably be the last action of our Ministry.

Dikshit and I, unlike the civil servants, were still puzzled that such a proposal as the CPSP card could even be seriously under consideration by the Health and Social Welfare Ministries. We can both see clearly that it is wonderful ammunition for the Opposition. I asked Mathur if the Health Ministry doesn't realize how damaging this would be to the government?

'I'm sure they do, Mantriji,' he said. 'That's why they support it.'

This was even more puzzling, since I had always been under the impression that the Health Ministry is in favour of family planning. 'Is it or isn't it?' I asked Mathur.

'Yes and no,' he replied of course, 'if you'll pardon the expression. The Health Ministry is pro-family planning because it is really anti-family planning. In fact the Administrative Service was united in its desire to make sure Family Planning didn't work. That's why we went into it.'

This sounded like a riddle to me. I asked him to explain further. And basically, his argument was as follows: India has had the same family planning objectives for at least the last thirty years—if the government started to impose a strict policy now, the electorate may get annoyed. At the moment, our population has crossed one billion and is growing every day. The more people there are, the more problems the country will face . . . and we will get a better chance to serve the nation . . . in other words, do nothing. And the Health Ministry can see no reason to change when it has worked so well until now.

I was staggered by all of this. I thought that all of us who are publicly pro-family planning believed in the social welfare motive. I said this to Mathur, and he simply chuckled.

So I asked him: if we don't believe in the social welfare motive, why are we pushing this card scheme?

'Same reason,' came the reply. 'The more schemes there are, the more arguments you can stir up, and the more futile and impotent it becomes.'

This all strikes me as the most appalling cynicism, and I said so.

Mathur agreed complacently. 'Ji Mantriji. We call it politics.'

I must say that, to me, it's all beginning to look suspiciously like a plot to get rid of me. Dikshit didn't subscribe to a conspiracy theory on this occasion, on the grounds that I'm to be got rid *of anyway* as my Ministry is to be abolished.

But I've got a sneaking suspicion that the PM just wants to make absolutely sure. Dikshit told me not to be paranoid, but I think *he'd* be paranoid if everyone were plotting against him.

'We're on your side, Mantriji.' Mathur was trying to be comforting. Life is full of surprises!

Then I had an idea. I suddenly realized that Mishraji will be on my side. I can't imagine why I didn't think of it before. He's Minister for Health—and, to my certain knowledge, Mishraji is genuinely pro-family planning (Mathur calls him '*buddhu*' [*simpleton —Ed.*]).

We've arranged a meeting with him. I can't think *how* he can help, exactly, but between us we may find some lever.

187

December 19th

All is well. The battle is won. My career, Mathur's career, and the MAA have all been saved by a brilliant piece of political opportunism, of which I am extremely proud. Plus a little bit of luck, of course. But it's been a very satisfactory day.

We all gathered conspiratorially at Mishraji's office. He was full of his usual second-rate witticisms.

'You've done a Samson act, Suryaprakash.'

I looked blank.

'You see, you wanted to reduce the Administrative Service, and you've done it. You've pulled the whole superstructure down—and buried yourself.'

I didn't know whether I was supposed to smile, or congratulate him on his wit, or what.

Mathur, of course, couldn't wait to join the analogy game. 'A Pyrrhic victory,' he intoned mournfully, presumably to remind us all that he is a classicist.

'Any ideas?' I asked Mishraji.

He had none. So we all had another of our tremendous gloomy silences.

Dikshit, fortuitously as it turned out, continued worrying away at the puzzle of why the PM wanted to introduce a CPSP card. 'I don't understand it. It doesn't make sense. Why can't the PM see the damage it's going to do to the government?'

I agreed, and remarked that this CPSP thing was the worst disaster to befall the government since I was made a member of the Cabinet. *[We don't think that Suryaprakash actually meant what he seems to be saying here —Ed.]*

Mishraji was quite calm about the CPSP card. 'Everyone knows it won't happen,' he said.

Who does he mean by 'everyone'? I certainly didn't know it

wouldn't happen—but then, I didn't even know it *would* happen till yesterday.

'The PM,' continued Mishraji, 'has to play along with it till after the UNFPA Prize is awarded.'

Apparently the UNFPA is the United Nations Population Fund Award, given once every five years. The PM is the frontrunner for this year's award. It's awarded to the statesman who has made the biggest contribution to Family Planning in Asia.

'The award committee meets in a month,' said Mishraji, 'and so obviously the PM doesn't want to rock the boat until it's in the bag.'

I think I caught Kaul mumbling to himself that you don't put boats in bags, but it was very quiet, I might have misheard, and he refused to repeat what he had said which makes me think I didn't mishear at all.

'And,' said Mishraji, reaching the point at last, 'once the prize is won, the PM will obviously ditch the CPSP card.'

I had this wonderful idea. I couldn't quite articulate it. It was slowly forming in the back of my mind. But first I needed some answers.

'Mishraji,' I asked. 'How many people know about the winner of the UNFPA prize?'

'It's top secret,' he said. Naturally, I was disappointed. Top secret means that everyone knows.

But not this time, apparently. '*Top secret,* top secret,' said Mishraji.

I was now so excited that I was becoming incoherent. 'Don't you see?' I said. 'Opposition MPs . . . leaks . . .'

And at that moment God was on my side. The door opened, and in stepped Raibabu. He apologized, and said he'd return later, but I stopped him. I told him that he was the very man I wanted to see, that I wanted his advice, and invited him to take a seat.

He pretended that he was eager to help me. But he warned that if it were a case of shutting stable doors after horses have bolted, even he would be powerless to help. I said, flatteringly, that I'm sure that he would not be powerless. I put it to him that I was in a serious moral dilemma—which, of course, I invented at that very moment.

My dilemma was this, I said. I told Raibabu that I knew that an Opposition MP was planning to table a question to the PM about whether or not the CPSP scheme is to be adopted by India.

He was immediately jumpy. 'Which Opposition MP? The CPSP scheme is top secret.'

'Like the winner of the UNFPA?' I asked. We eyed each other carefully—I wasn't entirely sure of my next move, but thankfully Kaul stepped in with an inspirational reply. 'I think Mantriji means a hypothetical Opposition MP,' he said. Good old Kaul.

Raibabu said that it was highly improbable that such a question would be asked.

I ignored that, and explained that if the question were to be asked, there were only two possible replies: if the PM says *yes* it would be damaging to the government in the country—but if the PM says *no* it would be even more damaging to the government in Asia. And to the PM personally—in view of the UNFPA.

Raibabu nodded, and waited. So I continued. 'Suppose a hypothetical Minister got wind of this hypothetical Opposition MP's question, in advance, what should he do?'

'The only responsible course for a loyal minister,' he said carefully, 'would be to see that the question was not tabled. That must be obvious.'

'It's a serious business trying to suppress an MP's question,' I said. Of course, he and I both knew that, as yet, there was no question and no such Opposition MP—but that there could be, if I chose to set it up.

'The only way to stop him,' I offered, 'might be to let the Opposition MP table a question asking the PM to squash rumours about the closure of the Ministry of Administrative Affairs.'

There it was. My offer of a deal. Out in the open. Raibabu paused to consider, just for a few moments, in case he could see a way out. But there was none.

And, to his credit, he handled it superbly. At once out came all the appropriate phrases: 'But I'm sure . . . whatever made you think? . . . No question of anything but the fullest support . . .' etc.

Then Mathur, who had got the idea at last, moved in for the kill.

'But you said only a few days ago that the plan to abolish the Ministry had been put up and the PM was smiling on it.'

'Smiling *at* it,' said Raibabu smoothly. 'Smiling *at* it, not *on* it. The idea was ridiculous, laughable, out of the question. A joke.' Beautifully done—I take my hat off to him.

So I asked him for a circular from the PM's office, to be circulated to all departments within twenty-four hours, scotching the rumour. So that we could all share the joke.

'Do you really think it's necessary?' he asked.

'Yes,' replied Mathur, Kaul, Dikshit, Mishraji and I. In unison.

Raibabu said that in that case, he was sure it could be arranged, that it would be a pleasure, how much he had enjoyed chatting to us all, excused himself and left. Presumably he hurried straight to the PMO.

191

Game, set and match. One of my most brilliant performances. I am exceedingly pleased with myself.

Kaul asked, after Raibabu had gone, if he can *really* fix it for us. 'Don't Prime Ministers have a mind of their own?' he asked.

'Certainly,' I said to Kaul. 'But in the words of a wise man, when you've got your head in the frying pan, you learn how to blow out the fire.'

7

Jaanne Ka Haq
(The Right to Know)

January 2nd

Today I had an environmental issue to deal with. A deputation of several environmentalists brought me a petition. Six fat exercise books, full of signatures. There must be thousands of signatures, if not hundreds of thousands.

They were protesting about my proposed new legislation to sort out all the existing confusions and anomalies in the present system—not that you can call it a system—which is a mess, a hotchpotch. Local authorities, the tourism department, the archaeological survey committee and the national parks are all backbiting and buck-passing and nobody knows where they are and nothing gets done. The sole purpose of the new legislation is to tidy all this up and make all these wretched committees work together.

I explained this to the deputation. 'You know what committees are?' I said. 'Always squabbling and procrastinating and wasting everyone's time.'

'We are a committee,' said one of them, an unprepossessing bespectacled female of indeterminate age but of clear upper-middle-class Delhi origins. She seemed rather offended.

I explained that I didn't mean her sort of committee; all that I was trying to do was create a new authority with clear simple procedures. Public money will be saved. It seems to me that it should be welcome to everyone.

However, these representatives of the Delhi middle class were worried about some place called Pahargarh. Apparently it is going to lose its protected status under the new scheme—like one or two other places—because it's simply not economic to administer it properly.

But it seems that Pahargarh is regarded by some of these socialites as a vital part of India's heritage. 'The monkeys have dwelt in it for generations,' spluttered an elderly upper-class socialite.

'How do you know?' I asked, simply out of curiosity.

'It said so in the *Indian Age*,' said an intense young man in chappals.

Some reason for believing anything! You've only got to be in public life for about a week before you start to question if the newspapers are even giving you today's date with any accuracy! However, the young man thrust a copy of the *Indian Age* at me.

I looked at the story he had circled in red. Actually, what the *Indian Age* said was: 'The monkeys have dwelt in it for generators.'

I read it aloud, and laughed, but they appeared to have absolutely no sense of humour. Then the middle-aged lady in a brown sari that enveloped mighty hips demanded, 'How would you feel if you were going to have office blocks built all over your garden by a lot of giant monkeys?'

Giant monkeys? I tried not to laugh at this Kadar Khan-esque vision [*Kadar Khan is a popular screen actor in Hindi movies with a flair for comedy — Ed.*], while another of these freaks continued self-righteously, 'There's nothing special about man, Mr Singh. We're not above nature. We're all a part of it. Men are monkeys too, you know.'

Obviously I knew that already. I had just come from Parliament.

Kaul helped me get rid of them after about ten minutes. I made no promises to them, and gave them the usual *pyar-ki-batein* [*actual: loving words, meaning: bullshit — Ed.*] about all views being taken into consideration at the appropriate stage. But I am concerned that no one in the Department warned me that the unified Master Plan for the administration of the rural areas would mean removing special protected status from these blasted monkeys. Not that I give a damn about monkeys, but I have been allowed to tell Parliament and the press that no loss of amenity was involved.

I should take this matter up with Mathur tomorrow.

I shall also take up the matter of why my time is being wasted with monkey business of this kind, when I want to spend much more time meeting junior staff here, getting to know their problems, and generally finding out how to run the Department more efficiently.

[*We discovered a remarkable exchange of memos between Shri Rajnath Mathur and Shri Kaul, written during this week —Ed.*]

MINISTRY OF
ADMINISTRATIVE AFFAIRS

From the Secretary

K.

I gather that Mantriji has been arranging for
himself unsupervised meetings with junior
members of the Department: Deputy Secretaries,
Directors, and even right down to Section
Officers. Please explain.

R.M.

2/1

From the Private Secretary

Mathursaheb
Mantriji wishes to get to know members
of the Department at all levels, and to
understand what they do and why.

K. Jan 2nd

From the Secretary

K.

These meetings must be stopped at once.
If Mantriji talks to underlings he may learn
things that we don't know ourselves. Our
whole position could be undermined.

R.M.
3/1

From the Private Secretary

Mathursaheb

Mantriji feels that such meetings increase knowledge. He also has expressed a wish to run the Department better, as things are now going pretty well.

<u>K. Jan 3rd</u>

From the Secretary

K.

I think you ought to be very careful. I am puzzled by your recent memos and am wondering if Mantriji is being entirely straightforward. I am bound to say that you should give urgent and active consideration to this matter, and ask yourself if you have considered all the consequences which could be unfortunate, or even regrettable.

R.M.

4/1

[*Translation:* 'Considered all the implications' means 'You are making a complete hash of your job'. 'Consequences which could be unfortunate, or even regrettable' means 'You are in imminent danger of being transferred to a remote district' —Ed.]

From the Private Secretary

Mathursaheb
I should be grateful for further advice
on this matter.

<u>K. Jan 4th</u>

From the Secretary

K.

Please note the following points:

1. *You refer to increased knowledge. Desirable and worthy though this ambition is, please remember that it is folly to increase your knowledge at the expense of your authority.*

2. *When a Minister actually starts to run his Department, things are <u>not</u> going pretty well. They are going pretty badly. It is not Mantriji's job to run the Department. It is my job, for which I have had twenty-five years training and practice.*

3. *If the Ministers were allowed to run the Department we should have:*

(i) *chaos*

(ii) *innovations*

(iii) *public debate*

(iv) *outside scrutiny.*

4. *A Minister has three functions:*

(i) *He is an Advocate. He makes the Department's actions seem plausible to Parliament and the public.*

(ii) *He is our Man in Parliament, steering our legislation through Parliament. (N.B. Ours, not his.)*

(iii) *He is our breadwinner. His duty is to fight in Cabinet for the money and budgets <u>we</u> need to do <u>our</u> job.*

PLEASE NOTE: It's not his function to review departmental procedures and practices with Deputy Secretaries and Section Officers.

R.M.

5/1

204

Kaul Saheb recalls:
Being rather young and nadaan [*green —Ed.*] at this time, I was still somewhat puzzled about how to put Mathursaheb's advice into practice, as Mantriji made these diary appointments for himself and was getting thoroughly on top of his work.

I sought a meeting with Mathursaheb, and began it by attempting to explain that I couldn't prevent Mantriji from doing what he wanted if he had the time.

Mathursaheb was thunderously angry! He asked me why Mantriji had free time. He told me to ensure that Mantriji never had free time, and that it was my fault if he had. My job was to create activity. Mantriji must make speeches, go on district visits, foreign junkets, meet deputations, work through mountains of files, and be forced to deal with crises, emergencies and panics.

If Mantriji made spaces in his diary, I was to fill them up again. And I was to make sure that he spent his time where he was not under our feet and would do no damage—the Parliament for instance.

However, I do recall that I managed to redeem myself a little when I was able to inform Mathursaheb that Mantriji was— even as we spoke—involved in a completely trivial meeting about preserving monkeys in Pahargarh.

In fact, he was so pleased that I suggested that I should try to find some other threatened species with which to involve Mantriji.

Mathursaheb replied that I need not look far —Private Secretaries who could not occupy their Ministers were a threatened species.

[*Suryaprakash's diary continues —Ed.*]

January 3rd
This morning I raised the matter of the threatened furry animals,

and the fact that I had told Parliament that no loss of amenity i.e. no problem was involved.

Mathursaheb said that I had told the House no such thing. The speech had contained the words 'no *khaas* [*significant — Ed.*] problem'.

I thought this was the same thing, but Mathur disabused me. 'On the contrary, there's all the difference in the world, Mantriji. Almost anything can be attacked as a loss of amenity i.e. a problem, and almost anything can be defended as not a significant problem. One must appreciate the significance of significant.'

I remarked that six books full of signatures could hardly be called insignificant. Mathur suggested I look inside them. I did, and to my utter astonishment I saw that there were a handful of signatures in each book, about a hundred altogether at the most. A very cunning ploy—a press photo of a petition of six fat books is so much more impressive than a list of names on a sheet of A4 paper. And indeed, the publicity about these monkeys could really be rather damaging.

However, Mathur had organized a press release which said that the relevant taluk is merely deregistered, not threatened; that monkeys are very plentiful all over the area; that there is a connection between monkeys and diseases; and which reiterates that there is no 'significant loss of amenity'.

We called in the press officer, who agreed with Mathur that it was unlikely to make the national press except a few lines perhaps on an inside page of the *Indian Age*. The consensus at our meeting was that it is only the urban intellectual middle class who worry about the preservation of the rural areas because they don't have to live in it. They just read about it.

So we had dealt satisfactorily with the problems of the animal kingdom. Now I went on to raise the important fundamental question: Why was I not told the full facts before I made the announcement to Parliament?

Mathur's reason was astonishing. 'Mantriji,' he said blandly, 'there are those who have argued—and indeed very cogently—that on occasion there are some things it is better for Mantris not to know.'

I could hardly believe my ears. But there was more to come. 'Mantriji,' he continued smoothly, 'your answers in the House and at the press conference were superb. You were convinced, and therefore convincing. Could you have spoken with the same authority if the wildlife activists had been driving you wild?'

Leaving aside this awful pun, which in any case I suspect might have been unintentional despite Mathur's pretensions to wit, I was profoundly shocked by this open assertion of his right to keep me, the people's representative, in ignorance. Absolutely monstrous. I told him so.

He tried to tell me that it was in my best interests, a specious argument if ever I heard one. I told him that it was intolerable, and must not occur again.

And I intend to see that it doesn't.

January 9th

For the past week Dikshit and I have been hard at work on a plan to reorganize the Department. One of the purposes is to have assorted officials at all levels reporting to me.

Today I attempted to explain the new system to Mathur, who effectively refused to listen.

Instead, he interrupted as I began, and told me that he had something to say to me that I might not like to hear. He said it as if this were something new!

As it happens, I had left my dictaphone running, and his

remarks were recorded for posterity. What he actually said to me was: 'Mantriji, the traditional allocation of executive responsibilities has always been so determined as to liberate the ministerial incumbent from the administrative minutiae by devolving the managerial functions to those whose experience and qualifications have better formed them for the performance of such humble offices, thereby releasing their political overlords for the more onerous duties and profound deliberations that are the inevitable concomitant of their exalted position.'

I couldn't imagine why he thought I wouldn't want to hear that. Presumably he thought it would upset me—but how can you be upset by something you don't understand a word of?

Yet again, I begged him to express himself in plain words. This request always surprises him, as he is always under the extraordinary impression that he has done so.

Nevertheless, he thought hard for a moment and then, plainly, opted for expressing himself in words of one syllable.

'You are not here to run this Department,' he said.

I was somewhat taken aback. I remarked that I think I am, and the public thinks so too.

'With respect,' he said, and I restrained myself from punching him in the mouth, 'you are wrong and they are wrong.'

He then went on to say that it is *his* job to run the Department. And that *my* job is to make policy, get legislation enacted and—above all—secure the Department's budget in Cabinet.

'Sometimes I suspect,' I said to him, 'that the budget is all you really care about.'

'It is rather important,' he answered acidly. 'If nobody cares about the budget we could end up with a Department so small that even a Minister could run it.'

I'm sure he's not supposed to speak to me like this.

However, I wasn't upset because I'm sure of my ground. 'Mathursaheb,' I enquired sternly, 'are we about to have a fundamental disagreement about the nature of democracy?'

As always, he back-pedalled at once when seriously under fire. 'No, Mantriji,' he said in his most oily voice, 'we are merely having a demarcation dispute. I am only saying that the menial chore of running a Department is beneath you. You were fashioned for a nobler calling.'

Of course, the *maska* [*flattery —Ed.*] had no effect on me. I insisted on action, now! To that end, we left it that he would look at my re-organization plan. He promised to do his best to put it into practice, and will set up a committee of enquiry with broad terms of reference so that at the end of the day we can take the right decisions based on long-term considerations. He argued that this was preferable to rushing prematurely into precipitate and possibly ill-conceived actions which might have unforeseen repercussions. This seems perfectly satisfactory to me; he has conceded the need for wide-ranging reforms, and we might as well be sure of getting them right.

Meanwhile, while I am quite happy to leave all the routine paperwork to Mathur and his officials, from now on I am to have direct access to all information as Minister of this department. Finally, I made it clear that I never again wished to hear the phrase, 'there are some things it is better for a Minister not to know'.

January 14th

Sunday today, and I've been at home the entire weekend. I'm very worried about Mishti [*Suryaprakash Singh's daughter, eighteen years old at this time —Ed.*]. She really does seem to be quite unbalanced sometimes. I suppose it's all my fault. I've spent little enough time with her over the years, pressure of work and all that, and it's obviously no coincidence that virtually all my successful colleagues in Parliament have highly acrimonious relationships with their families and endlessly troublesome adolescent children.

But it can't all be my fault. Some of it must be her own fault! Surely!

She was out half the night and came down for a very late breakfast, just as Chandni and I were starting an early lunch. She picked up the *Times* with a gesture of disgust—solely because it's not the *Express*, or *Indian Age*, I suppose.

I had glanced quickly through all the papers in the morning, as usual, and a headline on a small story on an inside page of the *Age* gave me a nasty turn. 'SINGH THE MONKEY KILLER,' it went. The story was heavily slanted against me and in favour of the sentimental socialites—not surprising really, every paper has to pander to its typical reader.

> **Singh admitted that removed protected status from Pahargarh Taluk could mean the end of the road for the monkeys. A spokesman for the Bandar Area Bachao Andolan (BABA) said: 'Singh has signed the monkeys' death warrant.'**

I nobly refrained from saying to Mishti, 'Good afternoon' when she came down.

However, I did ask her why she was so late home last night, to which she replied, rather pompously, 'There are some things it is better for a father not to know.'

210

'Don't you start,' I snapped, which, not surprisingly, puzzled her a little.

She told me she had been out with the Acts. I was momentarily sympathetic and suggested she see the doctor. Then I realized she meant the Student Activists. I had been slow on the uptake because I didn't know she was an Activist. Last time we talked she had been an Environmentalist.

'Uday's an activist,' she explained.

'Uday?' My mind was blank.

'You've only met him about fifteen times,' she said in her most scathing tone, the voice that teenage girls specially reserve for when they speak to their fathers.

Then Chandni, who could surely see that I was trying to work my way through five huge files this weekend, asked me to go shopping with her at Khan Market for the imminent wedding of a random niece. When I somewhat irritably explained to her about the files, she said they could wait!

'Chandni,' I said, 'it may have escaped your notice that I am a Minister of the Government of India. A member of the Indian government. I do a fairly important job.'

Chandni was strangely unsympathetic. She merely answered that I had thirty-five thousand civil servants to help me, whereas she had none. 'You can play with your memos later,' she said. 'The shopping's got to be done today.'

This was too much. So I explained to Chandni that only two days ago I won a considerable victory at the Department. And to prove it I showed her the pile of five red files stuffed full of papers.

She didn't think it proved anything of the sort. 'For a short while you were getting the better of Shri Rajnath Mathur, but now they've snowed you under again.'

211

I thought she had missed the point. I explained my reasoning: that Mathur had said to me, in so many words, that there are some things that it's better for a Minister not to know, which means that he hides things from me. Important things, perhaps. So I have now insisted that I'm told everything that goes on in the Department.

However, her reply made me rethink my situation. She smiled at me with genuine love and affection, and said: '*Pujya patidev* [*sarcastic Hindi for 'Darling husband'* —Ed.], how did you get to be a Cabinet Minister? You're such a *buddhu* [*Hindi for 'idiot'* —Ed.].'

Again I was speechless.

Chandni went on, 'Don't you see, you've played right into his hands? He must be utterly delighted. You've given him an open invitation to swamp you with useless information.'

I suddenly saw it all with new eyes. I dived for the files— they contained feasibility studies, technical reports, maintenance contracts, past papers of assorted committees, stationery requisitions . . . rubbish!

It's Catch-22. These fellows. Either they give you so little information that you don't know the facts, or so much information that you can't find them.

You can't win. They get you coming and going.

Meanwhile, still at the table, Mishti had been reading the story about the monkeys.

'There's a story about you here, Daddy,' she said accusingly.

I said I had read it. Nonetheless she read it out to me. 'Singh the Monkey Killer,' she said.

'Daddy's read it, darling,' said Chandni, loyally. As if stone deaf, Mishti read the whole story aloud. I told her it was a load of rubbish, she looked disbelieving, so I decided to explain in detail.

'One: I am not a monkey killer. Two: the monkey is not an endangered species. Three: the removal of protective status does not necessarily mean the monkeys will be killed. Four: if a few monkeys have to be sacrificed for the sake of a master plan that will save India's natural heritage—tough!'

The last part was a mistake, specially when said to idealistic, difficult teenagers always on the brink of a revolution for no reason. 'Why is it okay to kill monkeys?' cried my darling daughter. 'The end justifies the means, does it?'

Apart from the sheer absurdity of a teenager having the nerve to criticize someone else for believing that the end justifies the means—which I don't or not necessarily, anyway—she is really making a mountain out of a ridiculous molehill.

'It's because monkeys haven't got votes, isn't it?' This penetrating question completely floored me. I couldn't quite grasp what she was on about.

'If monkeys had votes you wouldn't be exterminating them. You'd be up there in Pahargarh, embracing them, reading them the *Hanuman Chalisa* [*an Indian religious text in praise of the monkey king, Hanuman —Ed.*], feeding their babies. Ingratiating yourself the way you always do. Yuck!'

Clearly I have not succeeded in ingratiating myself with my own daughter.

Chandni intervened again. 'Mishti,' she said, rather too gently I thought, 'that's not a very nice thing to say.'

'But it's true, isn't it?' said Mishti.

Chandni said, 'Ye-e-es, it's true . . . but well, he's in politics. Daddy has to be ingratiating.'

Thanks a lot.

'It's got to be stopped,' said Mishti. Having finished denouncing me, she was now instructing me.

'Too late,' I smiled nastily. 'The decision's been taken, Maharaniji.'

'I'm going to stop it, then,' she said.

Silly girl. 'Fine,' I said. 'That should be quite easy. Just get yourself adopted as a candidate, win a general election, serve with distinction in the Opposition, be appointed a Minister and repeal the act. No problem. Of course, the monkeys might be able to vote by then.'

She stomped out and, thank God, stayed out for the rest of the day.

[*Meanwhile, Shri Kaul was becoming increasingly uneasy about keeping secrets from Suryaprakash Singh. He was finding it difficult to accustom himself to the idea that civil servants apply the 'need to know' principle that is the basis of all security activities. Finally he sent a memo to Shri Mathur, asking for a further explanation as to why the Minister should not be allowed to know whatever he wants to know. The reply is printed opposite. —Ed.*]

From the Secretary

K.

This country is governed by Ministers making decisions from the various alternative proposals which we offer them.

If they had all the facts, they would see many other possibilities, some of which would not be in the public interest.

Nonetheless, they might formulate their own plans instead of choosing from the two or three which we put up.

So long as we formulate the proposals, we can guide them towards a correct decision. We in the Service are not foolish or misguided enough to believe that there is one single correct solution to any problem. However, it is our public duty to guide Mantriji towards what we like to call the common ground.

In order to guide Mantriji towards the common ground, key words should be inserted within a proposal to make it attractive.

Ministers will generally accept proposals which contain the words <u>simple</u>, <u>quick</u>, <u>popular</u>, and <u>cheap</u>.

Ministers will generally throw out proposals which contain the words <u>complicated</u>, <u>lengthy</u>, <u>expensive</u>, and <u>controversial</u>.

Above all, if you wish to describe a proposal in a way that guarantees that a Minister will reject it, describe it as <u>courageous</u>.

Remember, guiding Ministers in this fashion is what has made India what she is today.

RM.

15/1

215

[*It is worth examining Shri Rajnath Mathur's choice of words in this memo. The phrase 'the common ground', for example, was much used by senior civil servants after two quick changes in government in the 1990s. It seemed to mean policies that the Administrative Service can pursue without disturbance to the party in power. 'Courageous' as used in this context is an even more damning word than 'controversial'. 'Controversial' only means 'this will lose you votes'. 'Courageous' means 'this will lose you the election'.—Ed.*]

Sunday January 14th

Dear Daddy,

Day after tomorrow, I and my fellow student, Uday, intend to hold a twenty-four-hour protest vigil at Pahargarh, in aid of the monkeys.

On the Save-the-Monkeys vigil we will be wearing underwear only.

We shall put the announcement of this event out to the press and media if the monkeys' protection is not restored by 5 p.m. Monday January 15th, or some satisfactory assurance given.

We shall hold an almost-nude press conference at 6 p.m.

Mishti Singh

[*The above letter was found by Shri Kaul when he opened Suryaprakash Singh's papers in the office on Monday 15 January. The envelope was addressed to 'Daddy' but rules state that Private*]

Secretaries should open every letter of every classification up to and including TOP SECRET, unless specifically marked PERSONAL. This was a letter not marked PERSONAL. Suryaprakash's diary continues —Ed.]

January 15th
This afternoon seemed to last an eternity. I think it was one of the worst afternoons of my political life so far. However, I shall relate it from the start.

On my return from the Cabinet committee after lunch, Kaul and Mathur edged into the office looking extremely anxious. I asked if anything was wrong.

For the next four minutes they appeared to speak in riddles.

'Shall we say, a slight embarrassment,' said Mathur.

'How slight?' I asked.

First he rambled on about not wishing to overstate the case or suggest that there was any cause for undue alarm, but nevertheless . . . etc. etc. I told him to get on with it, he told me he had a confession to make, and I told him to make a clean breast of it.

'Not the happiest of phrases, in the circumstances,' he replied enigmatically. I still hadn't the foggiest idea what he was talking about, although it was soon to become only too clear.

But Mathur couldn't find a way to tell me the bad news. Extraordinary. First he said there was to be a twenty-four-hour protest vigil in Pahargarh, conducted by a girl student and her friend, a boy. I could see no problem in two irresponsible student types trying—and failing—to attract attention to themselves.

And like an idiot, I said so. (If there's one lesson I learned today it is not to shoot from the hip. Wait until you know the full facts before giving any response, if you don't want to finish up

217

looking like a complete fool.)

But I got an attack of verbal diarrhoea. 'Nobody's interested,' I said. 'Everyone's fed up with these crazy students. They're just exhibitionists, you know.'

'In this case,' remarked Mathur, suddenly becoming less enigmatic, 'they seem to have something to exhibit. It is to be a semi-nude protest vigil.'

This did seem to present a problem. It would clearly attract considerable press interest, and could even get onto the front pages of the tabloids. Regrettably, however, Mathur hadn't given me the full picture, so I went on and on talking, making myself seem more idiotic every minute. 'Really, I don't know what gets into these students. Appalling. Quite shameless. And it's their parents' fault. Don't bring them up properly, let them run wild and feed them all this trendy middle-class anti-establishment nonsense. Basically, middle-class *ki bigdi hui santanen* [*the spoilt kids of the privileged middle-classes —Ed.*].' Then I wittered on about the lack of authority nowadays, and how all this student anarchy is a shocking indictment of their parents' lack of discipline.

At this point Mathur was kind enough to reveal to me that the student's name was Miss Singh. For a moment I thought it was a coincidence. And then the truth hit home. I've never felt so foolish in my whole life. I'm sure (at least I think I'm sure) that Mathur didn't intend to make my humiliation as complete as possible. But he succeeded. And I'll get him for it one day!

After I picked myself up off the floor (in a manner of speaking), I expressed the hope that the press might not think it worth going all the way to Pahargarh, 300 km from Delhi. Even as I spoke I knew I was talking rubbish—for a story like this the press would go all the way to Mount Everest.

Mathur and Kaul just looked pityingly at me, and then showed me the letter.

I noted that Mishti was giving out the press release at 5 p.m. Very professional. Misses the afternoon papers, which not too many people read, and therefore makes all the morning newspapers. She's learned something from being a politician's daughter.

Then Kaul said that he thought he had better mention that Mishti was ringing up in ten minutes for an answer.

I asked how we could kill the story. Silence from them both. 'Advise me,' I said.

'What about a bit of parental authority and discipline?' suggested Mathur. I told him not to be silly.

'If you could make her listen to reason . . .' volunteered Kaul. I explained to him that she was a sociology student. 'Oh I see,' he said sadly.

Another long pause for thought. Then I suggested calling the police.

Mathur shook his head, and composed the inevitable headline: MANTRI SETS POLICE ON SEMI-NUDE DAUGHTER.

'I'm not sure that completely kills the story, Mantriji', he said.

We sat in one of our tragic silences. Occasional sighs filled the room. Then Mathur suddenly perked up. 'What if . . .' he said.

'Yes?' I said hopefully.

'What if . . .' he said again, '. . . I looked at the files?'

I'm ashamed to say that I completely lost my temper with him. 'Bloody marvellous!' I shouted. 'Is that what you get paid for? My daughter's about to get herself all over the front page of the papers and probably on TV as well, and all you can think of

219

is the files! Brilliant!'

He waited till I finished yelling. 'Nevertheless . . .' he said.

'They're all out there,' said Kaul, quickly indicating the Private Office. Mathur disappeared as fast as he could, before I could shout at him again.

Kaul and I gazed at each other in despair. 'I wonder what sort of angle they'll take?' I said.

'Wide angle, I should think,' said Kaul. I glared at him. 'Oh, I see what you mean. Sorry.'

All I could think of was the fun the Opposition was going to have with this, next time I had to face questions in Parliament. 'Does the proud father want to make a statement?' 'Is the Minister's family getting too much exposure?' 'Did the Minister try to conduct a cover-up?' Or even: 'Does the Minister run the Ministry of Administrative Affairs any better than he runs his family?'

I mentioned the last question to Kaul, because it is my weak point. I added bitterly that I supposed Kaul would want me to tell the world that Mathur runs the Ministry.

Kaul seemed genuinely shocked. 'Certainly not, Mantriji, not I,' he said indignantly. 'I am your Private Secretary.'

'You mean,' I enquired disbelievingly, 'that when the chips are down, you'll be on my side, not Mathursaheb's?'

Kaul answered very simply, 'Mantriji, it is my job to see that the chips stay up!'

[*This is, in fact, a precise definition of the Private Secretary's role* —Ed.]

At that moment Mishti rang in. She was on a mobile phone. I grabbed the phone. First I tried bluffing. 'I got your little note,' I said, trying to laugh it off. 'You know, for a moment I was taken in. I thought it was serious.' My little laugh sounded false even to me.

'It *is* serious,' she replied coldly. 'Uday and I are just going to ring PTA and ANI, and then we're off to Pahargarh.'

Then I grovelled. I begged her to think of the damage to me. She replied that it was the monkeys who were going to be exterminated, not I.

She's quite wrong about that! This could have been the end of a promising career.

It was clear that she was about to go ahead with her dreadful plan, because I couldn't change my policy on her account, when Mathur came running through the door waving a file. I've never seen him run before. He was saying something about a new development and asked if he could speak to Mishti.

He took the phone, opened the file and began to explain his finding. 'I have just come upon the latest report in the government's Wildlife Department file. It throws a new light on the whole issue.'

He went on to explain that, apparently, there is no monkey colony in Pahargarh. Apparently the wording of the report says: 'The last evidence of monkey habitation—broken branches, stolen household items etc. etc.—was recorded eleven years ago.'

Mishti was plainly as astonished as Kaul and I. I was listening in on the conversation. So was Kaul. She asked how come the newspaper had said monkeys were there. Mathur explained that the story about the poor monkeys had been leaked to the press, untruthfully, by a local property developer.

Mishti was immediately willing to believe Mathur. As far as the student activitists are concerned, property developers are the devil's representatives on earth. She asked for the explanation.

'The Local Municipal Corporation have plans to use the space in Pahargarh to build a new school for underprivileged children, but the developer wants to buy it for a commercial complex.'

'But,' interrupted Mishti, 'if it's protected, he can't.'

'No,' agreed Mathur, 'but nor can the Municipal Corporation. And he knows that, if they can't, they'll spend the money on something else. Then, in twelve months, he'll move in, show that there are no monkeys after all, get the protection removed and build his offices.'

From the complete silence, I could tell that Mishti was profoundly shocked. Then Mathur added, 'It's common practice among property developers. Shocking, isn't it?'

I had no idea Mathur felt this way about property developers. I had thought he rather liked them.

Mishti asked Mathur if there was any wildlife at all in Pahargarh.

'Yes, there is some,' said Mathur, looking through the file. 'It's apparently been used as a rubbish dump by people from the area, so there are lots of reptiles, and rats.'

'Rats,' she said quietly. Mishti hates rats.

'Yes, thousands of them,' said Mathur and added generously, 'still, I suppose they're wildlife too, in their way.' He paused and then remarked: 'It would be a pity to play into the developer's hands, wouldn't it?'

'I suppose it would,' she answered. Clearly the Save-the-Monkeys vigil was off!

Mathur added, with great warmth and total hypocrisy, 'But do let me say how much I respect your views and commitment.'

She didn't ask to speak to me again. She just rang off. The crisis was over as suddenly as it had begun. There was no way she was going to conduct a semi-nude *pehra* [*vigil —Ed.*] with lots of rats in the vicinity—other than the press, of course.

I congratulated Mathur profusely. 'It was nothing, Mantriji,' he said self-effacingly, 'it was all in the files.'

I was amazed by the whole thing. What a cunning bastard that property developer must be. I asked Mathur to show me the report.

Suddenly he became his old evasive self. He told me it wasn't awfully interesting. Again I asked to see it. He held it behind his back like a guilty schoolboy.

Then I had an extraordinary insight. I asked him if any part of the story he told Mishti were true, even mistakenly true. He claimed he didn't understand my question. So I asked him, again, clearly, if there had been one word of truth in that amazingly convenient story which he had just told Mishti.

He eyed me, and then enquired slowly and carefully, 'Do you really want me to answer that question, Mantriji? Don't answer hastily.'

It was a good question. A very good question. I could think of no advantage in knowing the truth, if my suspicions were correct. And a huge disadvantage—I would be obliged to be dishonest with Mishti, something I have never done and will never do!

'No,' I said after a few moments, 'um, Mathursaheb, don't bother to answer.'

'Quite so,' he said, as smug as I've ever seen him. 'Perhaps you would care to note that there are some things that it is better for a Minister not to know.'